TRAITOROUS TOYS

A COZY CORGI MYSTERY

MILDRED ABBOTT

Wings of Ink

TRAITOROUS TOYS

Mildred Abbott

for
Nancy Drew
Phryne Fisher
and
Julia South

Cover, Logo, Chapter Heading Designer: A.J. Corza - SeeingStatic.com

Main Editor: Desi Chapman

2nd Editor: Corrine Harris

Recipe and photo provided by: Rolling Pin Bakery, Denver, Co. - RollingPinBakeshop.com

Visit Mildred's Webpage: MildredAbbott.com

❀ Created with Vellum

Despite Watson's sensitive nose, and the smell of recently varnished floors, we spent the entire day in the Cozy Corgi bookshop. When the motherlode of all deliveries arrived before noon, the majority of the books were at least within the walls of my store, and I now owned more than an empty building. Progress!

After having the sign hung, the floors and walls refinished, and all of the bookcases installed, I'd thought my dream shop was becoming a reality. But with mountains upon mountains of boxes of books taking up most of the large center room, it finally began to feel real. And that realness doubled down. Transforming the place seemed nearly impossible, especially considering the timeline I'd set for myself, but even so, excitement thrummed. It was happening. Finally.

I spent the rest of the afternoon pushing boxes to the center of the smaller rooms that ran around the perimeter of the main floor. The more I worked, the more manageable it seemed. I already knew my favorite space. The corner room in the back left side of the shop. It was the one with the largest river rock fireplace. My uncles' store had a Victorian sofa and antique standing lamp with an ornate fabric shade I'd been eyeing. Those would go there, and it would be my mystery-themed room. Each little nook would have its own genre. The largest offshoot would be the children's book area, and while I was going to make every inch of the store as spectacular as I could, the mystery room was going to be just a touch more special.

By the same time next year, I'd have the entire shop decked out for Christmas. As it was, I used some of my illusive time to cut out paper snowflakes and tape them to the windows looking out on the tourists passing by. Next year, lights, trees, and maybe I could even brew some spiced cider for customers. But, for now, wonky snowflakes would have to do for holiday cheer.

"If you keep glaring at me like that, I'm going to leave you home tomorrow." I glowered at Watson, who peered up at me as I taped the final snowflake on the glass. His corgi eyes doubtlessly did a better job of glowering than mine. "It's not like you'd be unsafe. With the fortune I just paid for your dog run, the abominable snowman himself couldn't break in."

The threat to leave him home was an empty one, and we both knew it. Even with the Fort Knox of dog enclosures, I'd worry about him the entire day and get absolutely nothing done. Never mind the fact that since he'd waddled into my life a little more than a year ago, we'd been inseparable.

Watson's intense look was interrupted by a sneeze, a second one, and then he went right back to glaring.

"You know, buddy, the Cozy Corgi bookstore is named after you. We're going to have to work on your disposition before we have living, breathing customers."

I was fairly certain his brown gaze darkened. Watson was persnickety about which strangers he would allow to fawn over him.

A few seconds longer of our staring battle and I admitted defeat. We had both known I would. The only way I could change his disposition in the moment was to offer him a treat. And I'd already given him five since coming to the store a few hours ago. Since moving to Estes Park, Watson had steadily required more treats, and he was just a bit "fluffier" than was healthy. Not that I had much room to judge. My newest friend, Katie, was a baker, and I felt fairly certain she was intent on me buying an entire new wardrobe, with all the fresh carby goodness she continually shoved my way.

"Fine. You win. But this bookstore isn't going to put itself together, you know." I strode to the counter, slipped into my jacket, and grabbed my purse and an incorrectly delivered letter. It seemed I got someone else's mail every other day. I wondered how much of my own ended up somewhere other than with me. At least all the books had come to the right place.

I couldn't blame Watson. The smell of stain, varnish, and all the other chemicals used to refinish the wooden floors of the two-leveled shop a couple of weeks before had finally faded. We'd had an entire day and a half of getting the Cozy Corgi ready without runny noses and stinging eyes before the newly installed bookcases that filled nearly every room on the main floor had their turn at a beauty treatment. I was planning on opening the store in January, but that was only two weeks away. If I started stocking the books on the shelves too soon, I feared no one would buy them due to their absorbing the chemical smell.

After slipping on his leash, I stepped outside with Watson, paused long enough to lock the front door of the shop, and then began walking down the sidewalk. The two stores on either side of the Cozy Corgi had been candy shops, but now sat empty, waiting. While some of the stores had closed for the winter season, these were the only ones that felt desolate. I was certain it wouldn't last for long.

"One more stop, and then it's family dinner night."

Watson turned his unimpressed gaze on me again.

"Barry, buddy. You get to see Barry."

And with that, his eyes lit up and he gave a little hop. My stepfather was Watson's favorite human in the world, outside of myself. And there were times I wasn't entirely certain I outranked Barry.

Though it was barely four thirty in the afternoon, the sky was dark and only a small pink glow remained over the rim of the mountains. Snow fell in thick soft flakes, and while it was cold, there was no wind, so it was a crisp pleasant sensation. The weather mixed with the garlands, light-festooned streetlamps, and the ropes of glowing tinsel across the street made me marvel at my new life.

When we first moved to Estes Park from Kansas City the month before, I'd felt like we'd landed inside a snow globe. Now, with the holiday barely a week away, I was convinced we lived in a Christmas village. The sensation was compounded by the endless rows of shops on Elkhorn Avenue, all of which were either vintage fifties and sixties mountain style or those, like mine, that looked like small log cabins.

Within five minutes, we walked close to the end of the next block, and I checked the address on the envelope. The return address showed that it was from a Denver law office. There was no business name, but the numbers matched those under the silver script that read Rocky Mountain Imprints on the glass door.

A bell chimed as we walked in, and Watson let out an irritated snuff seconds before the smell hit— not overly unpleasant, and less harsh than what my own shop currently smelled like, but it was a weird mix of heat, plastic, and something I didn't have a name for. Endless racks of T-shirts and hoodies filled the store, and every inch of wall space was papered in square designs, ranging from cute forest animals, to Smokey Bear, to borderline risqué logos about hiking naked.

"Welcome, and Merry Christmas!" A cute blonde woman waved at me from behind the counter.

I nearly jumped at the sudden sound of her voice. I hadn't noticed her amid all the cacophony of fabric colors and images. Not to mention she was nearly pixie small.

"Thank you! And Merry Christmas to you." I motioned down at Watson. "I hope you don't mind that my dog is with me." Estes Park was extremely dog friendly, but Watson and I had encountered the rare shopkeeper who didn't appreciate animals in their store. In their defense, Watson tended to leave a cloud of dog hair wherever he went, as evidenced by every article of clothing I owned.

"Of course not!" The woman's bright voice was nearly as cheerful as a pixie. "He's adorable. We actually sell T-shirts for dogs." Her eyes narrowed as she inspected Watson. "He's... a basset hound, right? I don't think we have any of those, but I do a lot of the art myself. I can custom-design something for you. Maybe a basset hound wearing reindeer ears or something for the season?"

I shook my head and managed to smile instead of grimace. "Thank you, but no. Watson would murder me in my sleep if I tried to put clothes on him. Once in a while, he'll let me get away with a little scarf, but even then he gives me attitude for days after. And he's a corgi." A basset hound and a corgi both were

long and short, but really couldn't look more different, with basset hound ears nearly dragging the floor,
and a corgi looking for all intents and purposes more
like a chiseled fox.

"Well, if you change your mind, let me know. I'll
happily create something for a corky. I've never tried
to do anything with scarves, but it could be a fun
adventure."

A *corky*? I was going to have to remember that
one. Maybe that could be a new nickname when
Watson was being a snot.

As we walked closer to the counter, the woman
seemed to get smaller. Granted, that wasn't an
unusual sensation for me upon meeting petite
women. I was a healthy five foot ten, which seemed
like a good size to me, but anytime I was around
women the stature of my mother, I grew the tiniest
bit self-conscious. At thirty-eight, I'd expected to
outgrow that particular insecurity. Maybe by the
time I was forty....

"I am actually not here to shop. Sorry." I held out
the envelope. "This was delivered to my store by
accident. It's addressed to a Sarah M. Beeman, but it
had your shop's address."

The blonde's eyes narrowed as she took the envelope, and then she glanced toward the back of the

store before flashing me another smile. "Thank you. I'll see that she gets it." She cocked her head. "Wait a second. You said it was delivered to your store? I don't think I've met...." Her gaze left me once more, flicked to Watson, and then I saw understanding. "Ah! The Cozy Corky, the bookshop that's coming. I saw your sign. It's adorable."

She might not know her dog breeds, but with that comment, she won my approval. I was particularly proud of the wooden sign above my door with a corgi sitting on a stack of books. I held out my hand. "That's me. My name is Winifred Page, but everyone calls me Fred."

"Fred! That's almost as adorable as your shop sign." She slipped her tiny hand into mine. "I am Peg Singer." She tilted her head toward the back. "My husband, Joe, and I own the shop." She broke our hands' embrace and then gasped. "I have the best idea! That logo would be amazing on T-shirts and hoodies, we can even put them on hats. If you buy them in bulk, I'll give you a discount, and then you can mark them up and sell them at your store." She gestured behind her at a row of trophies. "Each summer we locals have a softball season. There were so many shop owners by the end of last year, we talked about splitting into two teams. You could lead the new one, and your little dog could be the mascot. Joe does really wonderful things with jersey imprints."

I shook my head, a little more emphatically than I'd intend. "I'm so not a sports person. Any team I'd be on would be guaranteed to lose. And Watson is about as athletic as a beached whale." I reminded myself I needed to get off to a good start with the other business owners, so I paused, considering. "The Cozy Corgi logo on shirts and stuff might be cute, though."

"I promise you it would be."

"Let me think about it, but...." I fished around in my purse for my newly printed business cards "Let me leave you my information and you can send me the details. Will that work?"

"Absolutely!" The card went the way of the letter. "I'll send you some options and quotes in the next couple of days."

I hadn't figured out what I was going to do with the top level of my shop, it had been an apartment before—and the scene of a murder. I hadn't wanted to extend the bookstore up there, preferring to keep it more of an intimate space, but maybe Cozy Corgi merchandise could be fun.

Watson pulled on his leash, obviously done with

another smelly location. I followed his lead. "It was a pleasure to meet you, Peg. We should probably get going, though. My little guy is getting hungry." I loved Watson for all that he was, even his often grumpy disposition. But one of my favorite parts of puppy motherhood was always having a ready excuse to leave.

"It was great to meet you as well, Fred." She gave a finger-wiggling wave to Watson. "And you too, Walter."

I truly did like the idea of the Cozy Corgi merchandise, but I made a mental note to double and then triple check spelling on any proofs she might send my way. The Cozy Corgi could easily end up being the Grumpy Goat or some such nonsense.

The snow had picked up, and as Watson and I stepped outside, the cold fresh mountain air was such a contrast to the plasticky smell of the T-shirt shop that I stood there for a second to luxuriate.

I turned back the way we'd come, and the store next to Rocky Mountain Imprints caught my eye. I wasn't sure how I'd missed it to begin with. Toys filled the window, and like my shop, the outside was a log cabin façade. The arched wooden sign over the door read Bushy Evergreen's Workshop. Unlike the T-shirt store, even from my spot on the sidewalk, it was easy to see the place was completely decked out for Christmas. I gave Watson an apologetic grimace. "One more stop before Barry. But this is the last one. I promise."

Before he could sit down and refuse to move, I pushed open the door and ushered him inside.

Sure enough, the place was as charming as it seemed from the outside. I'd toured all the stores when we first moved, but I'd been so focused on all the drama, I hadn't paid too much attention to aesthetics. Bushy Evergreen was an unfortunate name choice, but *workshop* was appropriate. It felt like Watson and I had stepped through a portal and landed in Santa's workshop in the North Pole. The tiny place practically overflowed with toys. For a second I couldn't figure out what was unusual about it, but then it hit me, only increasing the sensation of being in a place owned by Santa. Most of the toys— much like Estes Park itself—seemed to be from a time long ago. Tops, jack-in-the-boxes, wooden train sets and cars, and endless rows of stuffed animals. Many of the wooden toys and figurines looked expertly hand carved. In all the chaos of toys, three different Christmas trees were stuffed here and there, twinkling brightly. Garland was roped around every available surface, looping over the perimeter of the walls and outlining the shelves and tables.

"Wow." I stood in awe and forgot that I was nearly forty. This place was Christmas morning—smells of hot chocolate and molasses, the feeling of rushing down the stairs to find brightly colored packages under a sparkling tree.

There was a warm chuckle from somewhere to the left. "Never get tired of seeing that expression on people's faces. I don't think I've ever noticed one on a dog before, but even your furry friend appears enchanted."

I glanced at Watson. Sure enough, Watson's gaze flicked from one thing to another and he seemed captivated by it all, rather than irritated at keeping Barry waiting. Talk about a Christmas miracle. Maybe we really had stumbled upon Santa's workshop.

Catching myself, I looked toward the voice, and seemed to misplace my own. The man standing behind the counter was no elf. Nor was he Santa. He was a tall, rugged mountain of a man. Dark red hair and stunningly handsome. Where Peg had made me feel like a giant, this man made me feel like... well, probably how Peg had felt next to me, I assumed.

He flashed a bright white smile, somehow increasing his good looks, which shouldn't have been possible. "You all right?"

I nodded and had to lick my lips so I wouldn't drool, more than anything. I pointed to the garland strewn magically over the store. "Yes. I've just never seen garland that lights up before." That much was true, the crystalline garland was a constant shifting rainbow of colors. It almost looked like it was made from shards of glass or snow, and somehow glowed in countless sparkling hues.

His thick brows creased. "Yeah, it was my idiot brother's idea. Pretty spectacular stuff, unless you're the one hanging it. I think I bled for a week." Whatever irritation he felt vanished. "Looking for a gift?"

I shook my head. I was not looking for a gift. Although, since I was in a toyshop... "Yes, though I have no idea what to get. I have nieces and nephews. Two who are fourteen and two who are eight. Two boys, and two girls." He had a small dimple in his chin. Not too deep as to be distracting, but just enough to highlight how chiseled his jaw truly was. "Well, they're my stepnieces and stepnephews actually. I'm not very good at this whole aunt thing. My stepfather has two daughters; they're twins." His blue eyes might actually be made from sapphires.

"And of course they married twin brothers, because Verona and Zelda weren't identical enough, they had to marry twins. And they each have a fourteen-year-old and an eight-year-old, and I have absolutely no idea what I'm supposed to do for presents. Judging from the way they reacted the last few Christmases, I'm a horrible gift giver."

Watson yanked at his leash, pulling my attention to him. He cocked one of his puppy brows at me and sat down.

He'd just earned himself another treat.

If I'd kept going, I probably would've told the man my entire family history. I turned back to him but focused on a carved bear over his shoulder. Maybe he was like an eclipse, you could function if you didn't look directly at him.

"I can definitely help you out with the eight-year-olds, but I doubt we'll have much to offer the teenagers. They seem to want nothing more than cell phones, iPads, and cash." He gave another chuckle, proving that the sound of his voice was just as distracting as his appearance, no matter where I looked. "Depending on what they're into, I just got a new shipment of...." His voice trailed off momentarily, causing me to look him full in the face again. "Wait a minute. I recognize you, and your dog.

You're—" He snapped his fingers a couple times. "—Fred Page, the one opening the bookshop where the old taxidermy place used to be. Where Opal was killed."

For a moment I was beyond flattered that he had not only recognized me but recalled my name. Then I quickly realized chances were he'd been much more captivated by the murder and investigation that had swirled around me upon my arrival in town than he was about me personally. And that, more than keeping my focus away from him, helped me to quit acting like a complete fool. "That's me. For better or worse. Watson and I are the ones opening the bookshop. You must be... Bushy?"

Even as I said it, I knew it couldn't be. A man like that didn't have the name Bushy.

He shook his head, and once more there was a flash of irritation like there'd been about the garland. "No. This was my father's store originally. He still carves a lot of the toys, but it's mine now. Bushy Evergreen was one of Santa's original elves. He was a woodcarver and was in charge of the toyshop. My father felt a kinship with him. I would love nothing more than to put a sensible name on the place, but we've been here for over fifty years. Doesn't make good business sense to change it now." His charm was back. "My name is Declan, thankfully, not Bushy."

Before I had the opportunity to somehow put my foot in my mouth again, there was a slamming of a door, and a voice rang out from somewhere in the back. "Declan, you're never going to believe what I just found. I was just driving back from the grocery store and there was this old chest sitting beside a dumpster." A man rushed through the doorway carrying a wooden box that looked like it had been kept at the bottom of the ocean for the past century. At a glance, I almost thought he was Declan's twin, but it was a fleeting notion. He had the same height, coloring, and hair, but even though he had similar features to Declan, everything seemed off somehow —not malformed, just not as pleasing. Even so, he was very clearly related to Declan. "I was thinking I can clean it up, and Dad could—" His words fell away as he noticed me, and halted. "Oh, sorry. Didn't mean to be so loud. Didn't realize we had customers."

Two other figures emerged from the back. I wasn't sure if they'd been there the entire time or if they'd arrived with the strange Declan look-alike. An ancient-looking man with snowy hair, who was clearly Declan's father, and a raven-haired woman, who was just as beautiful as Declan. Both of them halted as well.

"Yes, imagine that. A toy store having an actual customer at Christmastime. Shocking." The coldness and shift in Declan's voice drew my attention away from the other three people. His handsome features were suddenly hard. But a heartbeat later, he was charming again, his voice warm and pleasant. "Might as well make introductions while we're all here. This is Fred Page, the one who's opening the new bookshop." He gestured from me toward the three individuals. "This is my father, Duncan, my brother, Dolan, and my wife, Daphne."

"That's a lot of Ds." I wasn't sure if it was the residual effect of Declan's stunning appearance or his abrupt shift from warm and inviting to cold and harsh, but whatever it was, I chose to say *that* instead of *hello, nice to meet you.*

Dolan gave a maniacal laugh, the father's brows knitted in an expression which reminded me of Watson in his grumpy moments, and Daphne smiled as she spoke. "That's true. I've often wondered if Declan married me simply because of my name. My mother-in-law's name was Della, believe it or not." She shrugged and patted her flat stomach. "We won't know if it's a boy or a girl until the little one arrives, but I can guarantee you the name will start with D."

Dolan let out another wild laugh. It wasn't exactly off-putting, but a little crazed or something. Actually there was something off entirely. I couldn't figure out what it was. I only knew that the Christmassy cheer of Santa's workshop had morphed into something else. And probably sensing it himself, Watson once again pulled on his leash, this time making it very clear he wanted to go.

"Well...." I attempted to force an easy-breezy tone, but was fairly certain I failed. "It's lovely to meet all of you." I refocused on Declan, this time not mesmerized by his appearance. "I'm running late for dinner with my family. Mom's making a big spread. I'll drop in before Christmas and find something good for the eight-year-olds."

And once more, Declan was all handsome charm and pleasant voice. "Please do. I'm sure we'll find something perfect for them. It was a pleasure to meet you, Fred. We'll look forward to visiting your store when you open."

"Thank you. I appreciate that." I gave a wave that hopefully encompassed everyone. "We'd best get going. Merry Christmas."

Dolan and Daphne responded as I turned and

hurried out the door. I paused in the cool air once more, but this time it wasn't refreshing. Just cold. I glanced down at Watson.

"What in the world was that?"

He didn't bother to respond, only took off down the sidewalk, pulling me with him.

Before I'd taken two steps, loud voices reached my ears, and I glanced through the window, past the toys, to see Declan shaking his fist as he yelled at Daphne. Dolan jumped between them, shouting something as well, though I couldn't make it out.

Duncan's old eyes met mine through the window and clearly told me to mind my own business.

I hesitated despite his stare, wondering what I should do.

With another tug on his leash, Watson made the decision for me.

By the time we got to Mom and Barry's house, we were running fifteen minutes late, and food was already on the table. As Watson and I walked through the door, all ten faces turned toward us.

My stepfather beamed. "Watson! My main man!"

Watson let out a loud bark, sounding more like a Doberman than a corgi, and took off like a shot. For being a little guy, he was strong, thanks to his herding heritage, and nearly yanked my thumb off as his leash trailed behind him. He crashed into Barry, who'd knelt from his chair like a long-lost lover.

My nephews and nieces giggled.

After making sure my thumb was still attached, I gave a little wave as I hung up my coat. "I know I'm second fiddle to His Majesty, but I'm here too. Sorry we're running late."

My tiny mother rose from her chair and hurried

to embrace me. "You're never second fiddle, dear. But do hurry over. The Tofurkey stew is getting cold, and you know it only resembles actual meat when it's hot."

Barry glanced up from his love fest with Watson. "Not true." Then he shrugged. "All right, it's probably true. I haven't had meat in a good three decades. What do I know?" He gave me a wink. "Good to see you, sweetheart."

I gave a quick round of embraces to Barry, my stepsisters, their husbands, and their four children before taking my seat beside Mom. Barry was the only vegetarian, and thankfully, for our new weekly family dinners, Mom also prepared a meat dish for the rest of us. Tonight's appeared to be lasagna.

Mom reached toward the pan with the spatula, then hesitated, glancing at Barry. "I almost forgot. Want to do the honors?"

He smiled and held his hands a couple of inches above the tabletop. As one, we grasped each other's hands completing the circle. "Mother Nature, thank you for all the nourishment and gifts you have provided. Thank you for the love and affection of family." His watery blue eyes twinkled. "And with the exception of Watson, who was made for such things, please forgive my family for devouring—" He glanced at my mom. "—what's in your pasta dish again?"

She sighed. "Beef, pork, and veal."

With a shuddering nod, he turned his attention skyward once more. "For devouring a mama cow, a pig, and a baby cow."

Zelda's oldest daughter giggled.

"Blessed be, peace on earth, and namaste." Barry released Mom's hand, signaling for the blessing to be done, then lifted a fork in the air. "Dig in, you murderers."

Even after six years of his marriage to my mother, I still hadn't been able to fully figure out where Barry stood on things. He was an adamant vegetarian, consumer of recreational marijuana, and wore only tie-dye shirts and loose-fitting yoga pants. I knew he was very sincere in his beliefs, but his strange prayer-like times I thought were more for show and to both humor and drive my mother a little bit crazy.

Sure enough, as she scooped a square of lasagna onto each person's plate, Mom gave an eye roll as she announced, "Here's your pig and baby cow. Eat it all or we'll never hear the end of it." She couldn't quite make it all the way through with a straight face, however.

And then the family was lost to the sounds of forks and knives on stoneware.

I also hadn't been able to make up my mind how I felt about our weekly family meals. This was only the third one since I moved to town. My stepsisters and their families had been on a cruise when I first arrived. On the one hand, the meals were somewhat comforting, the laughter and noise of people who love each other, a family. But it was foreign to me and at times felt a little chaotic and claustrophobic.

Dinners as a kid had been just as full of love and affection, but with being an only child, things were much quieter and calmer. Except for when my uncles came to visit. These larger family dinners always triggered an ache at the loss of my dad. Not that it took much. Even though he had passed seven years before, there were times when it felt like mere moments ago. I hoped he was looking down on us and smiling at the love my mom had found, and probably chuckling and shaking his head, knowing exactly how the disorder got under his only daughter's skin at times.

Distracted as I ate, I allowed my attention to wander over Mom and Barry's house, once more finding it both comforting and disconcerting to see Christmas decorations from my childhood combined with ones from Barry's life. The Christmas village that once belonged to my grandparents now spread out around the base of the tree, right next to a plastic elf wearing a fur-trimmed, tie-dyed suit. Barry had gleefully demonstrated how it danced to 'Grandma Got Ran Over by a Reindeer' when its ear was pinched. It was the only time I'd ever seen Watson annoyed with Barry.

A mix of pleasure and ache settled over me at the colliding of worlds. My past intermingled with my present. My childhood mementos that I'd shared with dad now side by side with this new life. Even on my tree at home, in my new-to-me cabin, decorations I'd made with Mom and Dad as a child hung next to corgi ornaments and a porcelain flamingo wearing a Santa hat from Barry.

All in all, it wasn't unpleasant. So many aspects of life crash together during the holidays. Time always seems to fold in on itself.

Coming back to the moment, my focus narrowed on the Christmas tree. Something seemed oddly familiar. Then, it clicked.

I motioned toward it with my fork as I addressed Mom. "Where did you get that garland? I just saw it for the first time today. It's amazing how it constantly changes colors."

Verona's husband, Jonah, angled himself from the other side of the table to look at me. "You must've been in the toyshop."

I nodded.

Before I could reply, Zelda's husband, Noah, piped up. "By next year every store downtown will have it."

Truth be told, I wasn't exactly sure who was Jonah and who was Noah. Even though I knew which husband belonged to which sister, when they weren't seated by their wives, I couldn't tell the identical twins apart. After knowing them for so many years, I supposed I should make more of an effort, but one set of identical twins marrying another set of identical twins just seemed to be asking for confusion, so I didn't feel too bad. At least with Barry's daughters, they were identical in every way except their hair—Verona being a blonde and Zelda a brunette. I was certain one of them colored her hair, but I'd never asked. My money was on Zelda, but, like their father, it wasn't smart to place a bet on anything either of the twins would do.

From the proud look on the brothers' faces, I did the math quickly. "Another one of your inventions?"

They both nodded, and one of them—goodness knew *which* one—explained. "We just took those

LED light strips and then made sleeves out of fiber-optic threads, like the ones we used to get at fairs and circuses and stuff. The first one took ages to make, but then we figured out how to mechanize the production. I could have sworn we told you about it a couple of weeks ago."

"I'm sorry. I'm sure you did. I've been so overwhelmed with trying to get my house together and the store ready for inventory that I probably forgot." Even though it was true, it was just an excuse. The twins had made a sizable fortune from their strange inventions. Each one came with endless filming of infomercials. They were nice guys, but it was all they talked about. Their constant string of failed and successful invention attempts blurred together. I doubted even their wives were able to keep it straight. "They're absolutely beautiful. Mesmerizing." Thinking back to what Declan had said, I spoke before I could stop myself. "I would imagine those would be hard to hang. If the fibers break, don't they stick in skin pretty easily?"

They both nodded enthusiastically, not daunted in the least. "That is an issue. One we're trying to figure out. Hopefully we'll have it all sorted by next season. But for now, we put a warning label on the

box and the instructions suggest the use of cattle-
man's gloves when decorating."

Zelda spoke from her place beside Barry, a
forkful of lasagna lifted halfway to her mouth. "Once
they fine-tune it, the boys are going to make gowns
for Verona and me for next year's New Year's Eve
bash." She smiled at me guiltily. "To be honest, I'm
not comfortable with their impact on the environ-
ment, but for a light-up gown, I'm willing to make an
exception for special occasions every once in a
while."

"I told you I'm not wearing that. It's socially and
morally irresponsible." Verona glared at her twin.
Though Barry hadn't even learned he had daughters
until they were in their twenties, the twins were a
testament of nature over nurture. Both of them were
female versions of their father's hippie, naturalistic
outlook on life. She smiled at me. "However, that
kind of dress would look lovely on you, Fred. I bet it
would make that long auburn hair of yours positively
glow."

I couldn't hold back a shudder. "Goodness, no.
I'd look like a walking, talking Christmas tree."

One of my nieces or nephews giggled. Not that I
blamed them.

"I still say the impact is low if we only do such

things on extremely special occasions. And I'm sure the boys could invent a way to recycle them. If nothing else."

"How is the house coming, Fred?" Barry cut off Zelda good-naturedly. Though Zelda and Verona were identical in nearly every single way, in the few areas they differed, it could be all-out war.

Even though I was with family, I was still uncomfortable being the focus of so many people at one time, but figured it was the lesser of the evils. "Mom was right. It was silly of me to have everything brought out here from Kansas City. I donated to Goodwill over half the things I paid to have driven out here." I gave a partial shrug toward Mom. "And you're right about not wanting all the things I had with Garrett in this new life. Once I get the store up and running, I thought maybe you and I can go shopping for some new items to replace things the ex-husband touched."

Mom shimmied her shoulders in pleasure. "Sounds wonderful, darling. And I'll buy a new bundle of sage to clear everything out again."

"That'd be great, Mom." The longer she was married to Barry, the more hippie she became. It was rather endearing. I gave a sweeping glance toward my nephews and nieces. "And speaking of shopping,

I am still getting the hang of buying presents for you all. I'd really appreciate Christmas lists this year. There was a beautiful assortment of carved wooden toys at Bushy Evergreen's Workshop, but even the owner thought I might want to shop elsewhere for you all."

Before the kids could reply, Zelda sucked in a breath and gave her sister a knowing look before turning back to me. "The owner? So you must have met Declan. Isn't he the dreamiest thing you ever saw?"

"Hey! Your husband is sitting right here!"

I glanced quickly at the twin who'd spoken. If he was Zelda's husband, that meant he was Noah. I made a mental note that Noah was on the right and Jonah was on the left. That would only help me until after dessert.

Zelda waved him off. "Oh hush, you know I adore you. And you're very handsome. But there's two of you, which means you're replaceable. There's only one of Declan Diamond."

I nearly choked. "Diamond? Are you kidding me?"

Zelda looked at me like I'd lost my mind. "No. Why is that strange? I think it's rather fitting for him. He sparkles like one."

"Declan Diamond?" How could she not see this? "I met the entire family. They all start with Ds." I listed them off on my fingers. "Duncan Diamond, Declan Diamond, Dolan Diamond, and Daphne Diamond, for crying out loud."

"Huh!" Verona smacked her sister's arm. "I never noticed that. Have you?"

Zelda shook her head as both their husbands looked affronted.

Barry chimed in, his voice solemn. "His face might be pretty, but that man's heart isn't."

"Barry!" Mom chided, her tone full of reproach. "That's a horrible thing to say. I know he isn't the nicest man, but—"

Barry shook his head in a rare act of disagreeing with Mom, and doubled down. "No, I mean it. He's an awful human."

I couldn't stop myself. The only aspect I'd inherited from my mother was her hair; everything else, including my curiosity, came from my detective father. And I knew just how rare it was for Barry to speak so vehemently against someone. "Why? What did he do?"

Before Mom could protest, Barry launched in. "Duncan and I went to school together back in the day. I watched him and his wife, the Lord rest her soul, build that toyshop from nothing to a beautiful success. Duncan working his fingers to the bone carving the most well-crafted and artistically sound toys and figures you could find anywhere. They spared no sacrifice for their two boys. Dolan's a little off, sure, but he's got the heart of an angel. Declan would sooner slit your throat than give you a five-dollar bill."

"Barry. Not in front of the kids." Mom tried again, but Barry was on a roll.

He nearly shook. I'd never seen Barry truly angry before, not even when he was falsely accused of murder. "Three years ago that ingrate had Duncan declared incompetent and took complete control of everything. The shop, the houses, the finances, everything. Duncan's little more than a poorly paid, hired hand in the very life he created."

"Granted, I didn't even hear Duncan speak, but he didn't seem incompetent in the few seconds we were together." Despite Mom's protests, I believed every word that came out of Barry's mouth. Especially considering the glimpse I had through the window. "How could that legally have happened? Didn't Duncan fight it?"

Barry shrugged, his anger slipping to an expression of confusion. "I honestly can't say. It still doesn't make sense. Gerald did everything he could, but it wasn't enough against Declan's high-paid Denver lawyer."

I barely caught myself before I let out a groan. "Gerald Jackson was Duncan's lawyer?"

He nodded. "Yeah, and he fought hard. It just didn't work. Duncan lost everything. Declan controls the entire family."

I cast a knowing glance at Mom, but she just shook her head. She knew better than to speak against Gerald Jackson. He was another of Barry's childhood friends. A nice man, I was certain, but a horrible lawyer. Mom wouldn't speak ill of most people, but having been the wife of a detective for so long, she knew incompetence when she saw it.

And poor Duncan Diamond, those grumpy, irritable eyes of his. Surrounded by his beautiful creations, and powerless.

One thing was for sure, Bushy Evergreen's Workshop was about as far from the actual Santa's workshop as you could get.

Thankfully, I'd made plans to meet Katie when she ended her shift at the coffee shop. If I hadn't, I probably would've thrown in the towel around two in the afternoon. As fun as it was to begin to see my dream come together, pushing box after heavy box of books from room to room was a bit backbreaking. Watson managed a good three minutes on the main level with me, and then disappeared upstairs to the kitchen. I figured he was continuing to look for the candy he'd found our first day in the building. That, or he was just letting me know he didn't appreciate being brought back here for another entire day.

At the scheduled time, Watson and I walked into Black Bear Roaster coffee shop just as Katie was hanging up her apron. She gave us a happy wave and elbowed the teenage barista with her elbow.

"Give Fred my employee discount on whatever she wants, please." She motioned toward the restroom. "I'll be right back. Just let me change out of my work clothes."

Knowing it was a mistake to consume caffeine so late in the day, I ordered my normal, a large dirty chai, and opted for a pumpkin scone. Whatever. I'd earned it.

By the time the chai was slid across the counter, Katie had joined Watson and me once more. Her brown, normally curly, shoulder-length hair had been pulled back into a short ponytail, and she gave me a quick hug and scratched Watson's ears. "Do you mind eating as we go? I've got to get out of here."

I cocked an eyebrow and intentionally leered at her sweater. "I'm not a fashionista by any means, but are you sure you want to go out in public wearing that?"

"Shut up!" She gave me a playful shove on my arm, causing some of the chai to spill, which Watson, being the helpful corgi he was, quickly cleaned off the floor. Katie motioned down at her purple sweater, which had an embroidered polar bear, giraffe, penguin, and mouse, all wearing Santa hats, on the front. "I don't think ugly Christmas sweaters should be relegated to ugly Christmas-sweater parties. It's not right."

I couldn't really say I agreed, but somehow it

made me adore Katie just a little bit more. "Even so, why are all the animals stacked on top of each other? Are they trying to see over something?"

"They're stacked biggest to smallest. Like a Christmas tree." Before I could point out that the stacked animals looked nothing like a Christmas tree, she pulled up the hem of her jeans and showed me her mismatched socks one at a time. "The right one is a cranky Christmas unicorn, and the left is the Grinch dressed up like Mrs. Claus."

Katie didn't usually remind me of Barry, but if he ever opted to not wear his tie-dye, this was exactly the sort of outfit he would concoct. "When I agreed to go Christmas shopping with you, despite detesting shopping, I didn't realize I was agreeing to Christmas dress-up."

She waved me off and then returned the favor of wardrobe commentary. "And surprise, surprise— Fred Page and baby-poop colors. Pea-green sweater over rust-colored broomstick skirt." Her eyes narrowed. "The only thing that makes me detest your color palette more is that you actually pull it off. Which shouldn't be possible." She cocked her head and then pulled back my hair in her overly familiar way. "You always have great taste in jewelry, however. You're tall enough to pull off long dangling silver earrings. On me, they would just make me look shorter." She slipped her arm into mine, once more providing Watson with a happy treat trailing behind us as she pulled me toward the door. "Now come on, before all the stores close."

Unlike the night before, though the sun was already setting, the late afternoon had clear skies and was only mildly brisk. The snow which had fallen that morning was still fresh enough on the heaps of cleared-away mounds that ran along the sidewalks to give a pleasant Christmas vibe when combined with lights winding up the streetlamps and making a canopy over the sections of Elkhorn Avenue between the rows of shops.

We passed store after store, with Katie doing no more than glancing through the windows. I couldn't tell if she was looking for something specific, or nothing at all.

"Who are we shopping for, anyway?" I used as benign a voice as possible. After a couple of questions about Katie's family, I'd caught on that it wasn't a topic she cared to discuss. And while I wanted to respect her boundaries, well... I was my father's daughter. I was curious.

If Katie noticed my double intent, she didn't let on. "No one, really. I just enjoy Christmas shopping.

I'm going to get my coworkers at the coffee shop some little tacky Estes Park souvenirs, just to be cute or something. And Carla, the owner, is having a baby in February. I haven't had a kid to buy for in years. So at least there'll be one cute present to get." She grinned up at me, a relaxed expression on her round face. "And I know you hate shopping, so I thought I might help you with your list."

That leading question hadn't garnered much information other than that at some point she'd had kids in her life to shop for. "I don't have a list, but if you want to do all my shopping for me, I'll happily give whatever you decide to buy. Even if it's ugly Christmas sweaters."

"Not a bad idea."

I took another bite of the scone and gave up. Hesitating, I studied Watson's pleading face. He was supposed to be on a diet. He let out a long whimper.

Whatever. It was Christmas. Weakening, like we'd both known I would, I handed the rest to Watson. We paused for the five seconds it took him to scarf it down.

"I really thought having you work at Black Bear Roaster would help their pastry items not to be dry. Every scone I've tried is almost tooth breaking."

"Nothing is made in-house. Everything Carla gets, she orders from a factory in Denver." Katie sighed wistfully. "When I mentioned that I'd be happy to make things at home and bring them in, she about had a conniption. Granted, I know it wouldn't meet health requirements, but it's killing me not being able to bake. It's making me miss working for Opal, as cantankerous as she was. Goodness, at this point I even miss Lois, even with her aversion for sugar. At least she had the sense to make things fresh."

I couldn't help but laugh. "You know you're a baker at heart when murder doesn't bother you as much as prepackaged scones."

Katie shrugged, unconcerned. "Not saying murder is good, but let's be honest. We've all met at least one person we've been tempted to try it out on. But processed food? That's just evil."

I started to make a crack about Katie's sweater and sock combo being evil when I realized we were walking in front of Paws. In a moment of panic, I hunched down to a squatted position and scurried, nearly crab-like, to the other side of the large window. Watson let out a startled yip. Upon reaching safety, I straightened once more, then realized Katie was no longer beside me.

She stood right in front of the pet store's window, staring at me. "What in the world was that?"

"Get over here." I motioned frantically at her until she complied. "The owner has two corgis, and he's desperate to have a playdate with Watson."

Katie glanced back at Paws. "What's wrong with playdates? Sounds like the cutest thing I can imagine. So cute that I might need to find a place that makes ugly Christmas sweaters for corgis, get the three of them together, and voila, I could have next year's Christmas card."

"Number one, something's off about Paulie. He's very nice, but there's something I can't put my finger on. Not to mention he named his corgis after those two eels in *The Little Mermaid* movie." I pulled the strand of hair that had blown in front of my eyes and tucked it behind my ear. "And two, you know that trying to wrangle Watson into a sweater would make Opal seem like an angelic cherub."

"Nah. Watson loves me. But even if he didn't, I'd just distract him with baked goods until I got him dressed." Katie motioned over her shoulder with her thumb. "And while we're listing things, my second point is that I want to see you do that every single year. It's our new Christmas tradition. All five foot ten of you scrunched down and scurrying over the sidewalk in plain view of all the tourists, thinking that somehow *that* made you invisible from the window."

I opened my mouth to argue, but then saw a mental picture of the scene she described and felt my cheeks burn. "Fine. Good point. It was just a moment of panic. Let's move along before Paulie truly does notice me."

"Sweetie, if he didn't notice that display, I think you're safe."

We finally went in a few stores, and Katie picked out horrendous knickknack after horrendous knick-knack. Boxes of chocolate-covered caramel balls labeled elk droppings, potholders with scantily clad park rangers on them, and pinecone owls with felt scarves.

"You know, everyone you work with already lives here, right? They won't actually want any of that."

"As if that's the point." After finishing the north side of the street, we'd paused and put the purchases in Katie's car, then began making our way up the south side. When we were directly in front of the Cozy Corgi, Katie held a gloved hand up to the window and peered in. "Wow! Look at all those boxes. You made a lot of progress today."

I'd nearly forgotten why my back was aching. "I

did. I think tomorrow's supposed to be a little warmer, so I'll crack open the windows and see if I can air the shop out some. Then maybe I can start shelving the books."

"It's going to be wonderful, Fred. I can feel it." Katie pulled back from the window, and we continued down the sidewalk. "Have you decided what to do with the second story yet?"

That consideration had been playing in the back of my mind all day. "I stopped in at the T-shirt printing place yesterday afternoon. The owner mentioned the possibility of putting my logo on T-shirts, hoodies, and hats and such. I can turn the top floor into Cozy Corgi merchandise. I was sort of thinking it was silly, but after seeing you buy a week's salary worth of junk about Estes Park, maybe I'm sitting on a gold mine and don't even know it."

She shrugged but lacked some of her typical enthusiasm. "Well, that's an idea, I suppose."

"Why? Sounds like you have a thought?"

Katie hesitated, then shrugged again. "No, and I'm sure some merchandise would be cute, but I don't think an entire floor of it would be the way to go." She was distracted for a moment as we passed a pizza parlor. "You know what, I think I'm almost done shopping. Let's make the toy store the final shop and then grab dinner. Sound good?"

"I get to be done shopping *and* eat? I knew you loved me." Plus, I'd get to be inside Bushy Evergreen's Workshop again. After Barry's history lesson the night before, I wanted to see what else I might notice.

"Great. I'll make it fast, and then—" She glanced back at me, her eyes widening, and then a goofy grin spread over her face as she pointed. "We might need to take care of that situation first."

I glanced back to see Watson squatting on the sidewalk, glaring at us for interrupting his privacy. "My fault for giving him the scone." Sliding my purse off my shoulder, I dug through, searching for the waste bags. Then I remembered I'd taken them out earlier in the day. But I'd left them on the counter. We were only a couple of stores down from the Cozy Corgi. I gestured toward the next block. "Why don't you go ahead? I left the bags at my shop. I'll go get one to take care of this and then meet you at the toy store."

"I don't mind waiting."

"No, go on. This means we get to dinner quicker."

"You sure know how to convince a girl, I'll give

you that." Katie gave a little wave. "See you in a second."

I paused to let Watson finish his business, and then we hurried back to the Cozy Corgi. The waste bags weren't on the counter. I started to do a quick search of the store, then realized they might've rolled anywhere as I was moving boxes, and with the tourists outside Christmas shopping, it was only a matter of moments before someone's shoe would turn the search into a moot point. I retrieved a large wad of toilet paper from the restroom, locked the shop back up, and rushed toward the ice cream parlor, moving quicker than Watson desired, practically dragging him.

By the time we got there, sure enough, the crisis was over and the damage done. Fearing that Watson's and my unintended victim was now inside the ice cream parlor glaring at us through the window, I hurried away once more, this time, refusing to give in to my new inclination to lower myself like a moron and rush out of view.

Once we were several stores down, I paused to glare at Watson, then reminded myself it wasn't his fault. I was the one slacking on motherly doggy duties. Watson was simply doing what dogs do.

"Well, they didn't kick us out of town when we

found a dead body in our shop. Surely dirtying a tourist's shoes won't be the deal breaker."

We crossed the intersection leading to the next block that held my uncles' antique store, Rocky Mountain Imprints, and the toyshop. When we passed Wings of the Rockies, I was tempted once more to crawl past the window. I had to break that inclination and quick! The owner of the wild-bird store and I weren't fans of each other. I hesitated at the door to the toyshop as I had a realization, then muttered conspiratorially to Watson. "We've only been in town a month, and if we count the ice cream parlor, there are already three locations we need to avoid. Maybe they *should* kick us out of town."

Watson simply stared after a second glance toward the door, as if asking what I was waiting for, didn't I know he was cold, and since when did I care about what people thought about us to begin with?

He had a point.

Shoving it all away, I pushed open the door, and we walked into the warmth of the toy store.

We made it about ten steps as we rounded the first tower of toys before halting. It took a moment for the scene to make any sense.

Declan was sprawled on his back in front of the counter. Katie was on her knees beside him, her fingers clawing at the ever-changing-hued garland that was wrapped around Declan's throat.

"Island of Misfit Toys" played in the background.

Watson whimpered.

A sense of déjà vu washed over me.

Another dead body. They really were going to kick us out of Estes Park.

Katie looked up at us, wild-eyed, her brown curls pulled free of the ponytail and whipping around her face. "Fred. Help me."

Her panicked tone broke through my shock. Dropping Watson's leash, I hurried toward her.

"I can't get it off. I can't get it off!" Katie's words were so rushed that they came out in the slur. Only then did I notice the blood on Declan's neck and on Katie's hands. I couldn't tell whose it was.

The garland. Noah and Jonah's stupid, sharp garland.

I changed course midway, nearly twisting my ankle in the process, and followed the trail of garland behind the counter. I yanked the plug-in out of the wall, causing the flickering lights to die, then glanced at the countertop. For a second, I didn't see what I was looking for, but then I found them sticking out of a cup full of pens. I grabbed the scissors and then joined Katie on the floor on the other side of Declan. "Can you pull it enough to get some slack?"

Katie stared at the scissors in confusion, and then understanding dawned and she nodded. "I think so." She pulled one hand free to make room, then used her other hand to create space between the garland and his neck, sucking in a breath as the garland made fresh cuts.

It was just enough for me to slide one of the blades through. Luckily the scissors were industrial quality, but even so it took forever. I had to practically saw through the layers of fiberglass, plastic, and wire. Maybe it took less than a minute, but it felt like hours as I worked with the scissors as Katie tried to pull the garland evermore loose.

And then it was free.

"Is he alive? I didn't even check. I just started trying to get it off him."

I held two of my fingers to the underside of his jaw and closed my eyes. After a few seconds, I shook my head. "No. We were too—" And then I felt it, barely there. Weak and faint but there. "Yes! He's alive."

Without thinking, I threw myself from the floor and grabbed the phone I'd noticed on the counter, then dialed 911.

FOUR

Officer Green's pale blue eyes narrowed in suspicion as she glared at me. "Why were you here again?"

From outside the toy store's windows, red light from the ambulance flashed across her face as it drove away, giving her a demonic appearance. To be fair, Officer Susan Green and I didn't have the best history, despite our limited interactions, so maybe it clouded my view of her.

"Like we said, Katie and I were Christmas shopping. We came in the store to purchase toys"—I attempted to keep the *duh* out of my tone, kinda—"for presents."

"Really?" Her cold gaze darted between Katie and me. "Katie Pizzala... Pozl...." She glanced down at her notepad. "Pizzolato."

"You can just call me Katie P." Katie tried for a smile. "Or just Katie, obviously."

Officer Green's lips tightened to such a thin

line that I was surprised she was able to speak. "Katie *Pizzolato*, you don't have any family in town. Who would you possibly be buying toys for?" Not giving Katie a chance to reply, she turned to me. "And the youngest kids in your family are eight years old. Are you telling me you're going to buy them an old-time metal top, or some hand-carved wooden blocks?"

I stared at her, impressed, despite myself. "You're very thorough, Officer."

"It's *my* town, Miss Page. I make it my job to be informed." She made a circling gesture with her pen, encompassing the toy store. "And as such, I know it doesn't make any sense for either one of you to come in here to buy toys."

My temper flared, and I barely stopped myself from saying that she was right. Katie and I got bored during our shopping spree and decided to strangle the owner of the toyshop to liven up the holidays.

Luckily, Katie piped up. "Carla, she owns Black Bear Roaster—"

"I'm aware who Carla is, Miss *Pizzolato*."

Katie flinched. "Okay, well, I work there now since—"

"I'm aware of that too, Miss *Pizzolato*. We've already established that I'm aware of what happens in *my* town." Officer Green seemed to be taking a bit too much enjoyment in every ounce of this.

Watson growled, drawing Officer Green's attention.

I took a step in front of him.

Remarkably, Katie just continued, her words coming out in a rush to finish before being cut off again. I had no idea how she wasn't screaming. "Since Carla is my boss and she's pregnant, I thought I'd get a baby gift here."

Officer Green opened her mouth, another argument coming, then gave a reluctant nod. "Oh."

She scribbled something on her notepad, then turned to me again. "And you? Please tell me your family isn't getting ready to produce any more offspring."

Despite my best efforts, I glanced toward some of the still-flashing garland on the shelves behind Officer Green. Instead of giving in to the impulse to add another strangling victim to the afternoon's events, I channeled my father. "Officer Green, we both know that you and my family have a tense relationship. It seems that it might be appropriate to have another officer do this questioning."

"I'm not questioning. This isn't an interrogation.

No charges are being pressed. I'm simply taking statements from witnesses." Somehow her sneer managed to deepen. "And as far as another officer, I'm sorry, but your boyfriend is out of town at the moment."

"Branson isn't my boyfriend." While there was definitely an attraction between us, and Branson had asked me out, we had yet to go on a date.

Her eyebrow cocked. "Either way, *Sergeant Wexler* is out of town." She smiled. "I'm afraid you're stuck with me. And I'd appreciate it if we could get back to the issue at hand. An attempted murder is more important than the status of your relationship with my so-called superior."

At that moment, another officer I remembered seeing at my shop last month cleared his throat and interrupted, holding up one of the large wooden nutcracker soldiers in gloved hands. "Officer Green, this was under that giant teddy bear." There appeared to be a red stain on the soldier's blue helmet.

Officer Green's eyes narrowed as she inspected the nutcracker. "Bag it." Then she turned back to Katie. "You still say you heard someone running when you walked into the store?"

Katie nodded. "Yes."

"You didn't see anyone hit the victim with anything? Didn't even see the strangulation begin?"

"Hit the victim?" Confusion flashed over Katie, but she pushed onward. "No. I told you. I came in the store, heard what I thought was running footsteps, and then found Declan on the ground, with the garland wrapped around his throat." For the first time, impatience sounded in Katie's tone. Or worry. I wasn't sure which.

Officer Green glanced down at Katie's hands and then mine. "And yet you're both covered in blood."

I followed her gaze. Somehow in the chaos, I hadn't even noticed. "Declan was bleeding. The garland was cutting into him, and into Katie's hands as she tried to get it off him."

Further disgust. How she managed to have so much was nearly miraculous. "Yes, I'm aware of the garland as well, Ms. Page. One more delight bestowed upon the world from your family."

"You weren't kidding. Even I wasn't aware the garland came from Noah and Jonah. There's no way I can keep track of all their inventions." The level of her knowledge of my family was a bit unsettling. It went beyond knowing her town, as she said. It was clear she'd been spending her time looking for something, some way to make life difficult for us. I didn't bother trying to keep my tone respectful. "You seem a little obsessed with my family, Susan. I don't think that's healthy. You might need to get some help for that."

Not helpful, Fred. Shut up!

Her shoulders straightened, and she took a step toward me. We were the exact same height and roughly the same build. But whereas I'd inherited my father's large bones, I was soft and curvy. Officer Green had turned her build into that of a weightlifter. It took every ounce of nerve I had not to flinch at the sight of her anger.

"Like I said. It's my job to keep this town safe. I know to keep vigilant. Even if Sergeant Wexler is distracted by... other things, I promise you I won't be." She took another step, close enough that I could smell her spearmint gum. "And on that note, you claim to have arrived late, after Miss Pizzolato supposedly discovered Declan just in time to conveniently interrupt a murder. If you were out shopping with your friend, why weren't you together?"

After too many years with a condescending husband, and then a betrayal from my best friend and business partner who stole my publishing house away from me, I was well equipped to handle being spoken down to by someone on a power trip. Officer

Susan Green seemed to always be on a power trip, at least where I was concerned. Once more, an endless litany of things I shouldn't say flitted through my mind and played over my tongue. So many that I had to bite my bottom lip.

"That shouldn't be a hard question to answer, Fred." Officer Green took a final step forward.

Watson growled again, and this time moved in front of me, baring his teeth.

Though I loved him for it, I yanked on his leash, forcing him behind. I had no doubt that given the chance, she would impound him or worse. The thought brought my tone back to respectful. "Watson... made a mess on the sidewalk, and I'd forgotten a waste bag. I had to go back to my shop to get one."

"Oh really?" From her victorious tone, I might as well have admitted I was the one who had attempted to kill Declan. "Can you offer proof that you picked up his refuse?"

"No...." I gaped at her, astounded at this line of questioning. "I... didn't get back in time. Someone had stepped in it."

Her blue eyes brightened for the first time, and she pulled out another pad of paper from inside her vest. "Well, I *hate* to have to tell you, but I will be writing you a ticket. Being a poopetrator comes with a hundred-dollar fine."

The idea that she was standing in the middle of a near-murder scene and worried about giving me a ticket for Watson's mess on the sidewalk should have been enough to make my head explode, but I was so astounded at both the use of her word *poopetrator* and her ability to utter it without so much as a smile that I was only capable of standing there in silence.

It seemed to be the final straw for Katie, however, who finally cracked. "Are you insane? Declan Diamond was nearly murdered, Fred and I barely managed to save his life, my hands are all cut up, we have no idea who was running away, and you're worried about dog poop? What is wrong with you?"

It would've been bad enough for Katie's outburst to prompt Officer Green to lose her temper, but the smile that spread across her face as she turned to look at Katie was so much more terrifying. "Right now, Miss Pizzolato, you are the only one talking about someone running away. Even your friend here can't vouch for you. The most obvious answer is typically the right solution. Perhaps after leaving hazardous waste on city property, Winifred Page accidentally interrupted your murder attempt, and you panicked.

That or she's attempting to cover for you. Poorly, I might add."

Katie's mouth hung open, speechless for a few moments. Then she blinked. "That makes absolutely no sense. Why would I try to kill Declan Diamond?"

Officer Green shrugged. "I'm less concerned with the why of the case, Miss Pizzolato, than I am the who." She refocused on her pad of paper and began jotting down something as she spoke. "Tell me again specifically what you hoped to buy when you came into Bushy Evergreen's Workshop."

The questioning continued for another half hour or more. By the time Katie and I were allowed to leave the toyshop, we were both trembling with rage and exhaustion. And I had a newly written ticket shoved in my purse.

We walked in silence until we reached the front of the Cozy Corgi and Katie glanced at the empty store to the right, where *Healthy Delights* was still painted over the window. "I'm so angry right now... It makes me completely understand how Opal died. I could club someone with a rolling pin, too."

I laid my hand on her shoulder. "Well, that makes two more reasons why we're friends. I feel the exact same way, and I know that I shouldn't admit that, but I'm going to anyway."

Katie let out a long shaky breath, and worry warred with the anger in her tone. "Should we be concerned? Officer Green will find any excuse possible to pin this on us. I don't know why she hates me so."

I didn't even have to consider that one. "She doesn't hate you."

Katie scoffed.

"Okay, yes she does. But not because of you. It's because of me. She's detested Mom and Barry for a long time. Her brother owns the magic shop. And Mom and Barry own the property. They're wonderful people, but you know what they'd be like as his landlords. Absentminded, scatterbrained, slow to follow through on everything. And I know her brother has tried to buy the shop multiple times, and Barry always refuses. Susan blames my family for both holding him back and, I think, just for being pains in general."

"Really? That's it? She is trying to pin murder on us just because of that?"

I shrugged. "Partly, yes. But I think there is also just a molecular dislike between us. I noticed it the first time she was questioning me about Opal, and it only got worse when Branson took over. I don't think she likes him, either. And knowing that there's some sort of attraction between the two of us, only makes her despise me more."

Katie sighed and sounded like she'd been awake for a week. "Well, I wish he was here."

"Me, too. Me, too." Branson had told me he was going to be gone a week or so, while insisting he'd take me to dinner before Christmas rolled around. But in the chaos in the toy store, I'd forgotten.

Katie brought my attention back from Branson. "What I don't understand is who would try to kill Declan? He owns a toy store, for crying out loud. You don't get more benign than that."

"Well... actually...." Judging from what Barry had said the night before, and from what I'd seen through the window, I could think of three people who might want to kill Declan. "How about we swing by the hospital to have them take care of your hands, then pick up a pizza, go to my house, and I'll fill you in?"

By the time Katie left, it was nearly nine o'clock. After hours of speculation and gossip, my anger had abated, but I was still unable to turn off my brain. I settled in the overstuffed armchair close to the fire, the Christmas tree sparkling from across the room in front of the window, and continued to reread my favorite Jacqueline Winspear novel. Before long, between the warmth of the book, the fireplace, and Watson at my feet, I dozed off.

The buzzing of my cell phone on the arm of the chair startled me awake. The fire was little more than embers, and a chill had entered the room. I glanced at the screen. It was nearly one in the morning, and though the number was unknown, the area code showed it was local.

I hit Accept. "Hello?"

"Fred!"

Katie's panicked voice made me sit up straighter, causing Watson to scurry away as I accidentally kicked out my feet. "Katie! What's wrong?"

"I've been arrested. They're saying I tried to kill Declan."

"What!" In my still slightly fuzzy brain, I wondered if she was kidding, but then I remembered Officer Green's expression. "Why?"

She sniffed. "My fingerprints were on that nutcracker guy they found."

"They were?" I hesitated. "Did you touch it?" Stupid question. Obviously she had if her fingerprints were on it. "And what does the nutcracker have to do with it?"

"I guess so, I must have, right? But I don't even remember that thing. I've never liked those. They're saying he was hit on the head with it, before being strangled, I guess. All I remember is walking in, seeing Declan's body, and trying to get that stupid garland off of him. But maybe... all I can think of is maybe it was in the way so I moved it, tossed it aside. I don't remember. It was all a blur."

I tried not to let my own panic take over. Whatever was going on, it could be figured out. "Okay, where are you?"

"At the police station." Katie's tone said that should've been obvious. "They arrested me. You're my one phone call."

I had to process through that. "Katie, why in the world would I be your one phone call? You should call your lawyer."

"Lawyer?" Katie's voice spiked. "I don't have a lawyer! What normal person has a lawyer? I don't even know a lawyer. And even if I did, I can't afford them. They said they're going to provide me one."

"Oh, Katie." I couldn't hold back a groan.

"What? I can't!"

I knew exactly which lawyer would be provided.

Even if there were a slew of them to choose from, both chance and Officer Green would make certain Gerald Jackson would be the one called. "Okay, well, I'm sure whoever they send you is better than nothing. But don't say too much. I'll get you a better one tomorrow, as soon as I can figure out who a better one is." Although *any* lawyer would be a better one. Not that I was going to say that to Katie at the moment.

"Fred, I didn't call to talk about lawyers." Some of the panic seemed to fade from Katie's voice, and she almost sounded relaxed. "I called for you. I need *you*."

"Why? What can I do? I'm not a lawyer."

Again, Katie sounded like the reason should be apparent. "Obviously I can't trust what the police are going to do if Officer Green has it out for me. I need you to work your magic."

"My magic?"

"Good grief, yes, Fred. Your magic! You're the one who cleared Barry's name when he was accused of killing Opal." She softened to nearly a whisper, making me wonder if someone was listening in. "I need you to figure out who did this."

After an almost sleepless night, I knew where to start. Even though I was still new to town, I was fairly certain I'd already discovered the biggest gossips among the shopkeepers. Gossip seemed to be the best bet. I didn't know much about Declan or the rest of the Diamond family, other than what Barry had told me, but if he was nearly as horrible as Barry said, I was willing to bet there were plenty of stories about Declan. My first thought was Anna and Carl Hansen, who owned the home decor shop. My initial impression of them had been their business owner-ship was little more than a front so they could be in the center of the hubbub at all times. But they were down the street and across the block from Bushy's, while the runners-up in the gossip competition were a mere few doors down. So they were the winners.

First things first, though. After a bad night, I needed caffeine. Although, that was really just an excuse. I could sleep twelve hours and still need caffeine to function. As Watson and I walked toward the Black Bear Roaster, I had to admit something to myself. Only part of my tossing and turning had been worry over my friend. There was plenty of that. I hated the thought of Katie spending the night in a cell, hated that she was caught in the middle of another murder drama just a few short weeks after the first. The same could be said for myself, I knew. And I needed to quit thinking of it as a murder investigation. Declan was simply unconscious, not dead. For that matter, I needed to quit thinking of it as an investigation. I wasn't the police. I was an ex-teacher turned ex-publisher turned bookshop owner who was also the daughter of a police detective. That was all.

But that was the other reason I'd been unable to sleep, not just worry over Katie, but a tingle of excitement. The realization made me feel guilty. I shouldn't be feeling anything like that, and not only because of Katie. A man was almost killed, and part of me felt like I'd been handed an early Christmas present. This wasn't a pretty little puzzle I had to put together. It was serious. Life and death. One that wasn't even my job to do.

And yet....

I glanced at Watson as I opened the door to the coffee shop, and he peered up at me, eyes wide and bright. At least one of us was fully rested, if his soft snores throughout the endless hours had been any indication. "Your mama needs therapy or something."

Watson seemed to consider, then flared his nose at the scents drifting our way, and led me inside.

He was right. Might as well focus on the task at hand. And if I was finding enjoyment over what Katie had asked me to do, so be it. Maybe I was simply getting a thrill by trying to help my friend.

Before I could mock myself for that thought, Carla spotted me from behind the counter, gave a big wave, then ushered me over. Despite my caffeine addiction, I'd never met her before, but judging from her expansive belly, I didn't need to be an actual police detective to determine who she was.

"You're Fred, right?"

I nodded. "Yes. And this is Watson. You're Carla."

She flashed a half smile, then leaned toward me across the counter, as much as she was able. "What in the world is going on? I got a voicemail from Katie this morning, letting me know she wouldn't be at work today. I had to drag my ever-expanding girth outta bed before dawn. She said something had come up and she'd explain to me when she came back in." Carla gestured over my shoulder toward the slew of customers. "But everyone's talking about her being arrested for trying to kill Declan Diamond."

For a heartbeat I debated lying, or at least playing coy. I wasn't certain why Katie hadn't just been upfront in the message, but it wouldn't do any good for me to play along at this point. "That's true." I decided to bend the truth, just a touch. Doubtlessly Carla would pass along anything I said, so maybe it would help some of the rumors die down. "She and I walked into the toy store yesterday and found Declan on the ground. Someone had tried to strangle him."

"Strangle?" Carla's eyes grew wider. "I heard that she bashed Declan over the head and he's in a coma."

Good Lord. That sentence alone made me miss the city, where you could wander around for an entire day and not bump into anyone you knew. Katie had been arrested in the wee hours of the night, and already the town was talking about how she was an attempted murderer. How in the world did people know about Declan getting hit on the head? Katie and I hadn't even known that at the time. As soon as the thought crossed my mind, I knew the answer. Obviously Susan Green was enjoying letting *her* town know all about Katie Pizzolato. I leveled my gaze at Carla, making sure to keep my tone firm yet friendly. If I sounded the least bit defensive, I would only make matters worse.

"I can guarantee you, she did not bash Declan over the head. Nor did she try to strangle him. The only thing Katie did was try to save his life, which she did."

"Oh!" Carla gave a tiny flinch and sounded a little bit chastised despite my effort at neutrality. "Oh, well then. That's... good of her." Carla passed a hand over her belly. "I'm glad to hear it. She's a sweet girl, a little odd, but likable, I suppose. A bit evasive when people try to get to know her better, especially around family."

I knew that much to be true. She didn't talk about family even with me. But I hadn't found it too big of a concern. Not everyone had a great family life. Despite our growing closeness, we'd known each other little more than a month. Not enough time to trust me with whatever hurts she might have. That Carla thought she was owed those details as Katie's new boss was nearly enough to make me turn Watson around and head to the other coffee shop clear across town. Then I remembered the quickly growing number of shops I was avoiding. I couldn't add another to the list.

"Well, I can promise you, Katie is not a murderer. And her family life doesn't keep her from being an excellent barista and employee." Might as well go for gold; it might help Katie out when she returned. "Plus, I can attest personally that she's one of the best bakers I've ever known. She could probably triple your business."

From the grimace that crossed Carla's lips, I knew it was a losing battle.

Before she could say anything else, I decided to make my order. It was clear any information I might get from Carla would be of the pure speculation variety. At least the gossip Anna and Carl—and my uncles—dealt in seemed fact-based. "I'm sorry to cut this short, but I really must get going. Would you mind getting me a large dirty chai and one of your pumpkin scones?" Maybe it would be softer first thing in the morning. If not, it looked like Watson would be breaking his diet yet again.

A few minutes later, Watson and I were back outside. I thought I'd hop into my Mini Cooper and drive the two blocks to my uncles' antique shop, but instead I decided to walk. If I really was going to be digging around, trying to figure out who might have it in for Declan Diamond, I needed to make myself a little more present among the other shopkeepers and definitely stop avoiding them. Even so, when I was close to Paws, I hurried Watson to the other side of the street. I considered it a win that I didn't attempt another crabwalk.

Before giving Watson the other half of the dry pumpkin scone, I double-checked to make certain I'd put waste bags into my purse. Luckily for him, I had, and he voraciously enjoyed his second breakfast.

I spared a glance into the toyshop as we passed. The door was locked, and the windows dark, like I'd expected. Another wave of guilt cut through me. Regardless of how I felt about Declan, his wife, his *pregnant* wife, had to worry about her husband dying at Christmas. I hadn't even thought of her in that way—as a wife, expectant mother, someone who loved her husband and was now hurting.

Of course, none of that was true if the other ways I had been thinking about her were accurate. All through the night, I'd speculated on motives for why she might try to kill him. Just from the brief flash I'd seen through the window two nights before, their marriage definitely wasn't without strife. Then again, lots of marriages were less-than-perfect and didn't result in murder, but maybe the brother who'd stepped between Declan and Daphne? The father Declan had pushed aside and taken his business and freedom? Maybe even a combo of the three?

Well, it wasn't my job to worry about Daphne and how she might be feeling. That was what the rest of her family was for. My job was to try to figure out.... I shook my head at the thought as I pushed open the door to my uncles' antique shop. No, it wasn't my job to find out who tried to kill Declan. But I was going to do it anyway. Katie was right. I'd helped to clear Barry's name and I *would* clear hers.

"Bless my soul, Fred and Watson. My day just got better." Gary smiled at me from where he knelt on the floor with a box of tools open at the base of a lamp. He issued a deep groan as he pushed himself from his knees to a standing position. At over six foot and maintaining the heavy muscles of his pro-football years, even at the age of sixty, he dwarfed me as he wrapped me in a hug. "Always good to see you, sweetheart."

"You too, Uncle Gary." And it was. Even though Gary was my uncle through marriage, he always brought to mind my father, with his deep voice, strong body, and calm, unshakable demeanor.

After releasing me, he gave Watson a quick pat

on the head then refocused on me. "You're either here because you decided to get the sofa and lamp for your shop, or you're snooping around trying to help your friend."

If Carla knew about Katie, no part of me was surprised Gary knew as well. "Both, actually. Though any help you might give me on Katie is more important than the antiques, of course."

"No niece of mine is going to say *anything* is more important than antiques." My mom's brother, Percival, rounded a corner in their maze-like antique shop and shook his finger at me. "Even if murder is involved, or attempted murder, in this case." Though he was the exact height as his husband, the two of them couldn't be more different. Percival was a decade older, and his wispy stature was the antithesis of Gary's bulk. He gave me a warm hug, then leaned his face close, pointing to his balding head. "Give your uncle a kiss, darling. We're under the mistletoe."

I had no idea how I'd missed it, but sure enough, he'd donned a headband with a long spring at the center and a sprig of mistletoe bobbing over us both. With a chuckle, I gave him a quick peck on the lips before he bent to pat Watson.

Watson let out a growl and backed up, his wide eyes startled as he stared at the waving mistletoe.

Percival gasped and stood up, offended. "Well, I never. See if you ever get a treat from me again, little one."

And at that word, I could see the war raging in Watson. Kill the alien creature floating above Percival's head or get a treat. To my shock, murder won. Watson growled again, this time showing his teeth.

I pointed toward the mistletoe. "You may want to give him a little space. I don't think Watson's a fan of your headband."

Understanding dawned in Percival's eyes, but he lifted his chin. "Well, he'll have to get with it. Fashion is fashion." He cast an accusatory glance at my salmon-hued broomstick skirt, but uncharacteristically kept his mouth shut. "Thankfully, he's a corgi, and I know he's part super sleuth like his mama, but even he can't reach up here."

"But I wish he could." Gary bugged his eyes out at me. "I've been waiting for that stupid headband to fall apart for twenty years. I'm pretty sure it's going to outlive us both."

Percival smacked Gary's arm but turned his attention to me. "So what's this I hear about something being more important than antiques? You can't tell me that sofa and lamp aren't going to be absolute perfection in your cozy little bookshop."

"No, you're right. I can't. I was just telling Gary I've decided to take both of them. I'm going to put them in the mystery room, the one with the river rock fireplace, like you suggested."

"Well, of course you are, you brilliant woman. You wouldn't make any other choice." Percival smiled in satisfaction. "Now if you'd just listen to me about your wardrobe...."

I laughed, repaying the smack on Gary's arm with one of my own. "I knew it would be too good to be true for you to keep your opinions to yourself."

"Pretty sure a man wearing a mistletoe headband has no room to talk about your wardrobe, Fred." Gary cast a sidelong glance at Percival, then smiled at me warmly. "You look beautiful as always. I think your hair has grown longer. Mountain life must be agreeing with you."

I normally kept my hair a little lower than my shoulder blades, but it had gotten long, especially on the days when it went from curly to merely wavy. And with the lack of humidity, this was happening more than it had in Kansas City. "I think it is. I really do love it here. Despite the crime rate."

Percival snorted. "Darling, I'm afraid we're going

to have to blame that one on you. You walk into town, and we have our first murder in years, and now an attempted one." He cocked his head. "Although, I suppose that isn't true. We just didn't know about some of the other murders."

"Speaking of, you said you weren't here just for the sofa and lamp. So fill us in." Gary motioned toward the sofa that would soon be in my shop. We crossed the space, and Percival and I sat on the sofa, with Gary taking a seat in an ornate armchair at its side.

I unhooked Watson's leash so he could explore and get away from Percival's mistletoe. "That's actually what I wanted from you. To fill *me* in. I only met Declan and his family once, two nights ago. And at first I found him very charming. But by the end, I'd changed my mind. And from what Barry tells me, my second impression was the correct one."

"If your first impression was that the man was a gorgeous, stunning, ravishingly handsome man, my darling niece, then you would be correct." Percival made a fanning motion with his hand in front of his face.

Gary rolled his eyes. "And if your second impression was that he was a selfish, egomaniacal narcissist, then you would also be correct."

"Well, nobody's perfect." Percival shrugged and gave a nod that was probably supposed to come off as wise. "All those things can be said just as truly about endless ugly people. If you're going to be evil, you might as well look good doing it."

"Evil? You really think he's evil?"

To my surprise, though it hadn't been his claim, Gary nodded. And while it was completely in Percival's nature to exaggerate, it wasn't true for Gary. "Why? Because of what he did to his father?"

"Oh, so you do know. Though that makes sense since you spoke to Barry." All humor left Percival's voice as his eyes darkened. "Duncan was never the most cheerful of people. Even as a kid, everyone said he had the soul of an old man. But he was kind, even if a little abrasive. And one of the best wood-craftsman I've ever seen. Besides when he lost Della, having his no-good son steal his business out from under him was the most devastated I've ever seen a man."

"Devastated enough to kill his own son?"

Gary and Percival both flinched, and it was Gary who responded. "You really are your father's daughter, aren't you? No beating around the bush and right to the point."

Percival didn't wait for me to respond. "No. And

maybe that's the problem. No matter what Declan did, Duncan could never hurt him, not even spank him. Those two boys were his weakness. Even Della said so. He spoiled them both rotten. I know Dolan's a bit of a strange bird, but he turned out fine despite it all. Declan didn't."

I decided to push a little more. Percival was right. That had been my father's approach—direct and upfront. I knew it wouldn't always work with the people in town, but I wasn't trying to manipulate my uncles. "Then what about Dolan or Daphne? If Declan was so evil, surely both of them had plenty of reasons to want him gone."

Both men shook their heads. Percival's voice stayed serious. "No way would Dolan do such a thing. I've known him since the day he was born. He didn't get his brother's looks or his father's talents, but he got his mother's kind heart. You couldn't ask for a sweeter man. And Daphne?" He shrugged. "Granted, I don't know her very well, but every interaction I've ever had has made me think she truly does have it all. Just as stunningly gorgeous as Declan and as sweet as Dolan. Her only flaw is her husband."

Maybe she decided to get rid of her only flaw. I didn't say that. As trustworthy as Gary and Percival were, it seemed they had a blind spot in regards to the Diamond family. Which, considering the connection went back for almost the past seventy years, at least for Percival, I suppose that made sense. "What about other people? Maybe Declan wasn't evil just to his family."

Gary pointed at me. "And that's what I was thinking. You're onto something there, Fred. I don't know if Declan managed to screw over anyone as royally as he did his own father, but it's well known you can't trust the man in business. He's cutthroat. Which, honestly, has helped the toyshop. The fellow who runs the pet shop tried to open a toy store when he came into town. Declan brought all the fires of hell down around him."

Percival sniffed. "Good enough, I say. There's something not quite right about that guy. He seems better suited to be around animals than children."

Even though there was only one person they could mean, I had to make sure. I'd planned on avoiding the pet shop until a last resort. "Paulie Mertz? The guy who owns Paws?"

Misreading my tone, Percival lifted a finger in my direction. "Now don't get defensive. I know he owns two corgis and all you corgi people stick together, but there's something there, even if I can't put my finger on it."

"I agree, actually. Though I can't picture him going up against Declan, not that I've had much interaction with either man."

"Nah, you've the measure of both of them I'd say. The pet shop guy folded so fast you would've missed the entire thing if you'd blinked." Gary shrugged. "Not that I could blame him. Declan can be an intense adversary if you cross him. He's a snake. Of course, that depends on who you ask. He's charmed most every woman in town. At least those who let their eyes do their thinking for them."

It took me a second to catch Gary's implication, but when I did, a huge portion of the town opened up as possible suspects. "Are you saying he's a bit of a womanizer?"

"A bit?" Percival cackled, his brightness returning. "The man has had so many affairs he might as well run for political office!"

And that would point back to Daphne. Get back at a cheating husband. Though physically, I couldn't see it. Declan was massive, strong, and healthy. Daphne was small, feminine, and pregnant. If he'd truly been hit in the head hard enough to put him in a coma, I couldn't quite picture her managing such a feat. But maybe.... "Were some of these affairs with married women?"

They both nodded.

A cuckold husband would definitely have the motivation. And the strength. Even if I couldn't figure out who it was, maybe I could find something to prove that motivation. Enough to clear Katie's name.

That brought the other reason I was here. "While we're at it, I need some advice. As you know, they have Katie in custody on suspicion of Declan's attempted murder, even though she's the one who saved his life."

"Ridiculous. The Green family have always been a barrel of idiots." Percival shook his head in disgust, and Gary didn't disagree.

I didn't know the rest of the family, and I didn't like Susan Green, but she didn't seem like an idiot to me. If she were, I'd be a lot less worried about her.

"Even so, she's managed to get Katie into a mess. If we were in Kansas City, I'd know who to call, but I don't know here. Who's a good lawyer in town, or even down in Denver who I could trust with Katie's case?"

For the first time, Percival looked utterly confused. "What do you need that for? I talked to

Gerald myself this morning. Told me all about it. He's in Katie's corner."

I spared a quick glance at Gary, who bit his bottom lip and gave a small shake of his head.

Some defensiveness had slipped into Percival's tone. "I know he's a little left of center, but so am I. He's a good lawyer. He'll do right by Katie."

I sighed, knowing that arguing would get me nowhere. "Well, I'm glad to hear it."

It was a marvel to me. I'd seen the good-old-boys-club effect countless times in my life. And as free-thinking and liberal as Barry was, I could understand his loyalty to Gerald. I'd expected different from Percival somehow. The three men and my mother had all grown up together; I guess grown up with Duncan Diamond too, come to think of it. Despite her unwillingness to speak ill of most people, my mom was the only one who was prepared to raise doubts about Gerald Jackson's capabilities. But somehow, even with these men I adored, the good old boys club was in effect—binding, and apparently, blinding as well.

Unclear if it showed just how much I adored Katie or if it merely proved I relished playing detective, I left my uncles' shop and headed directly to Paws. I'd planned on avoiding it entirely, unless for some reason it came up as a last resort. I wouldn't call my uncles' story about Paulie a last resort at this point, but it was definitely a lead.

Unlike most of the other stores I noticed when Katie and I were Christmas shopping, as Watson and I walked into Paws, we weren't greeted by the scent of cinnamon, clove, pumpkin, or any of the traditional scents of the holidays. While it didn't seem unclean, it smelled exactly like what it was. And from Watson's perked-up reaction, it appeared he approved. Even with my human nose, I could make out cedar chips, dog food, and the musky odor of rodents. I was certain, to Watson's heightened senses, it was a smorgasbord of scents. And above it all, combined with the manic melody of piped-in "Rockin' Around the Christmas Tree," were the loud screeches of parakeets, the gurgling of fish tanks, and the whirl of hamster wheels.

Before Watson made it to the counter, Flotsam and Jetsam came bounding from the back like overgrown Christmas chipmunks who'd overdosed on coffee beans. One of them wore a Santa hat with a jingling bell in place of the snowball, and the other had on an elf hat complete with pointed ears. Whichever one was wearing the Santa hat stumbled over a dog toy in the aisle, caught himself, and arrived at Watson a few seconds after the other. Watson stiffened but allowed the two shameless dogs to paw at him playfully and pull on his ears.

Unlike many of the corgis I'd met, Watson didn't have an overly playful nature, nor did he appreciate it in other dogs. Typically, if another dog tried to play with him, Watson would growl, back against my legs, and make it very clear if I didn't get him out of the situation soon, he'd hold me personally responsible for the rest of our existence. However, for whatever reason, if the dog was another corgi, even if he didn't play along, he managed to grin and bear it. Well, not so much grin. Watson had arrived in my life a little over a year ago, and I wasn't certain if whatever life he'd had before had turned him into a little bit of a sourpuss and grump, or if it had been his nature to begin with.

"Fred! Watson!" Paulie Mertz followed the path of his corgis and emerged from the back corner of the store, which was lined with fish tanks. At the sight of him, my mouth fell open, but I managed to catch my reaction quickly enough, or at least I thought so. The small thin man wore a clearly fake Santa beard and elf ears that matched the ones on his corgi. "I've been waiting for you to drop by. Every time I knock on your bookshop, no one ever answers. Even when I've seen your little cute orange car in front of it. I've been trying to schedule our corgi playdate."

"Oh, I'm so sorry, Paulie. Chances are I was either working on things upstairs or getting inventory arranged down in the basement." A complete and utter lie. Thanks to the large picture windows that looked out from either side of the front door, I had noticed Paulie headed my way, and I'm not too proud to admit that I hid—every time.

And at that moment, I quit blaming myself for the crabwalk in front of his window and searched desperately for a topic completely unrelated to corgi playdates, then realized they were plentiful.

"That's quite a beard you have on there. I didn't

realize you got into the spirit of Christmas quite so emphatically." Ridiculous thing to say, considering I'd managed to talk to the man for a grand total of ten minutes. Like I knew anything about him.

He offered a yellow-toothed smile. "I can take it or leave it, truthfully. Christmas is little more than commercialism and gross consumption." He offered a self-sacrificing shrug. "I do it for the boys. Flotsam and Jetsam have quite the holiday spirit, as you can see."

Right then, one of them nipped at Watson's nub of a tail. My little grump sat down promptly, utterly failing to tuck what little tail he had away. He glared up at me.

"Yes, they seem to be very much in the... frantic frenzy of it all."

Paulie nodded, seemingly completely unaware of Watson's and my discomfort. "Watson doesn't look like he's in the spirit of things at all. I have a reindeer costume in the back, even have antlers. I can get it so he doesn't feel left out."

"No, don't, but thank you." I tried to keep my voice pleasant. "He'd murder us both."

Paulie furrowed his brow as he inspected Watson. "Yes, I can see that." He bent down to scratch Watson's ears, and though Watson attempted to pull away, with

Flotsam and Jetsam trapping him on either side, he was forced to endure Paulie's affection. "You have Ursula's disposition, don't you?" He started to laugh and then broke it off abruptly. "No, you're not evil. More like King Triton. He wouldn't let Ariel have any fun."

I didn't even try to stop myself from looking around the shop to see if he had any of Noah and Jonah's garland hanging about. Somehow I'd forgotten the man's obsession with *The Little Mermaid*, despite his corgis being named after the sea witch's eels.

It was time to pull the trigger, before Watson lost his patience or I began to seriously consider plausible substitutions for the garland. "Sorry to drop in and run, Paulie, but I actually have tons to do today. If I'm to open the store by New Year's, I shouldn't be allowed out of the shop until I get the books shelved."

Paulie perked up, a cheerful expression over his poorly bearded face. "The boys and I would love to help. We're very good workers. We'd get the job done in half the time." His tone changed somewhat. "And with the extra time, we could always grab dinner after."

Luckily, this time I could rely on the truth to set

me free. "To be honest, I'm a complete control freak. I want to make sure every book is exactly so-so. I'm afraid by the end of trying to help me, you'd think I was the worst person in the world."

His face fell. "Ah, well, I understand."

There was such sincere loneliness in his tone that I couldn't help but feel bad. Nor could I bring myself to change my mind, whether or not that made me a horribly selfish person.

"Actually I just wanted to pop in—" I couldn't simply lead in with prying him for information. Not after hurting his feelings. "—and get another bag of that dog food you sold me last month. Watson just loved it."

I was pretty certain Watson understood a lot of what I said. But the fact that he didn't throw back his head and howl in laughter proved some things escaped him. The very thought that he would lower himself to eat dry dog food, no matter that it was a hundred dollars a bag, was nearly sacrilege. I'd been tossing some of the dry food out each morning for the chipmunks and squirrels in the trees beside my cabin.

Paulie perked up. "Wonderful! Let me get that for you." Then he was gone. Unfortunately, his two eels... er... corgis stayed behind, not giving Watson a respite.

A few seconds passed before there was a loud groan and a loud bang, followed by more parakeets screeching.

"Fred?" Paulie's embarrassed voice drifted from some unseen aisle. "Would you mind giving me a hand?"

I'd forgotten I'd had to help him the first time as well. Sure enough, when I rounded the corner to the dog food aisle, I found him struggling to pull the medium-size bag upright once more.

"Sorry, Paulie, I should've remembered. Here. Let me give you a hand." Sidestepping Flotsam and Jetsam, who were bookending Watson as he stayed at my feet, I bent down, and in a smooth motion tossed the bag of dog food onto my shoulder.

"I'll, yes. That... works too."

From the embarrassment that once again cut through Paulie's voice, I knew I'd messed up again. The least I could've done was to take one end of the bag and pretend I needed his help.

We crossed back to the counter, and indeed, I could've used his help as the three shifting corgis at my feet nearly caused me to stumble twenty times. And from the occasional soft gurgle from Watson's throat, I knew, whether Flotsam and Jetsam were corgis or not, our time was limited. I pulled out my credit card and decided to make it fast, after all. I wasn't sure if direct would work on Paulie Mertz like it did with my uncles or not, but it would have to do. "So while I'm here, I'm sure you've heard about what went on with Katie and me last night."

His brown eyes widened, and he nodded, a feverish glint growing in them. "With that Declan Diamond character. Yes, I heard."

There was no denying the glee in his tone, proving what Percival and Gary had said was true, not that I had ever doubted them. But combined with his expression, I finally put my finger on part of the reason Paulie Mertz gave me the willies. What my uncles had said was true, corgi people tended to stick together. Despite our differences, there was some almost unnamable quality that linked us. Something positive. Whatever that thing was, something about Paulie Mertz left me feeling uncomfortable. I almost felt guilty for it, but I'd learned to trust my instincts, even if I couldn't put my finger on why.

I took a heartbeat to make sure my tone stayed neutral. "Yes. That. And it seems like the whole town has also heard Katie was arrested for trying to kill him. And I can assure you, that isn't the case."

This time the glint in his eye was a little less malicious, possibly even holding a level of admiration, though I couldn't tell. "I heard you were the one who found out what happened to Opal. Does that mean you're looking into this for Katie?"

One of the eels accidentally nipped my ankles going for Watson's paw, and I jumped with a little yelp.

Paulie didn't attempt to call them back. Without asking, I snagged three of the large dog bones from the glass jar on the counter, tossed two of them to different sides of the room, and handed one to Watson. Sure enough, Flotsam and Jetsam went running. I refocused on Paulie. "I wouldn't say I'm looking into it. That's not my job, obviously; that's up to the police. I simply own a bookshop." Maybe it was my new perspective associating him with a rat, but the last thing I needed was him going around town saying I thought I was better than the police. "I just happened to hear a rumor about you and Declan, actually."

And with that, all awkwardness seemed to fade away, leaving him cold and hard. "I don't think I like what you're implying, Fred."

"What I'm—" His meaning solidified quickly. "Oh, no. I didn't think you had anything to do with it. I mean you couldn't even—" I started to say couldn't even lift a medium-size bag of dog food, but caught myself, thankfully. "—hurt a fly, I'm sure. You own corgis after all."

And like that, the warmth was back. Not warmth exactly but something akin to it. "Oh, sorry. Honestly, I've been waiting for someone to make that accusation. It's hardly a secret that Declan and I don't get along. I thought we were going to be friends. We were on the same softball league last summer when I moved to town."

"*You* were in a softball league?" I hadn't meant to say that, nor let my surprise slip out.

If he was offended, Paulie didn't let it show. "I was. You should consider joining, especially if Declan's not there. A lot of the shop owners do. Peg and Joe Singer from Rocky Mountain Imprints. Rion Spark, who owns a wedding dress shop, Pete Miller, the glassblower. Mark Green, who owns the magic shop. Even his sister, the cop. It's a great way to meet people if you're new and want to make friends. At least it's supposed to be."

If I didn't already find the idea of playing softball revolting, doing so alongside Susan Green and her brother sounded like a death wish. I didn't want to be anywhere near her when she had a bat in her hands.

Paulie had thrown so much information at me that I had to refocus to get back on track, which was also hindered by Flotsam and Jetsam being finished with their dog bones and once again pawing at Watson. "I hadn't heard about the softball team, but I did hear that you originally wanted to open a toy shop, but Declan... had other ideas."

He snorted. "That's one way to say it. He threatened me if I didn't open a different kind of shop."

"He threatened you? Physically?"

"No." Paulie shook his head. "Legally. Said he'd take me for everything I had. Even though there was nothing in the town ordinances saying there could only be one toy shop in town." He leveled his gaze at me. "Though, there is now."

"Really?" Despite myself, I leaned toward him. "You're saying he has such pull that he got them to change some of the town statutes?"

He shrugged, as if suddenly playing coy. "Estes Park is a great little place. But they like their own. Trust me, you'll find out soon enough, I'm sure. The town council has some very good people on it, so I've heard. But also has a couple who make sure the few natives left do better than the rest."

Now that was news. None of my family had mentioned that. Although, they wouldn't, would they? If it was true, they might not even be aware. Despite my mother being gone for a few decades, she was still a local. I'd had a very easy time with licensure and cutting through the red tape for opening my bookshop. Maybe that was because, even though I wasn't native, I was close enough?

That bit of news didn't have an impact regarding Declan's attack; he and his family were natives. But perhaps he'd pulled the same stunt with other new business owners in town. And one of them decided to fight back?

Watson let out a loud yelp at my feet and finally gave in and growled, baring his teeth at the two obnoxious corgis. I couldn't bring myself to scold him. In truth he'd done much better than I had. I shoved one of the corgi eels with my foot, drawing attention to me, as I signed the receipt Paulie offered me. "Well, Paulie, despite what it took you to get here, it seems like the pet shop really does suit you."

"Yes, it does." With the smile he gave, some of his rat-like appearance faded again. "Blessing in disguise, unanswered prayers, all of those things. I'm really happy here. At least with the shop."

Again his loneliness was evident in his tone, leaving me uncomfortable and still a touch guilty. I threw the bag of dog food over my shoulder once more. "Thanks for your time, Paulie." I patted the bag. "And for this. We should get going. Lots of work to do."

I'd almost made it to the door before he called out. "What about that corgi playdate? I'm a little busy myself, but I have a bit of time Saturday evening. How about then?"

Proving that I'd inherited just a touch more from my mother than auburn hair, I couldn't bring myself to deny him in his obvious loneliness. "Sure. But it will have to be quick. I simply have so much to do."

The brilliant smile that beamed from him erased all rodent similarities from his appearance, save for his yellowed teeth. "Oh, that is wonderful. I'm so happy. Flotsam and Jetsam will just have the time of their lives!"

"Yes, I'm sure they will." Even as I waved good-bye, I was trying to think of a way out of it. "See you Saturday."

After tossing the hundred-dollar bag of squirrel food in the trunk of my Mini Cooper, I got two burgers from Penelope's to go, and Watson and I made our way to the scenic area behind the south side of the shops, where the river ran. The city had recently revamped the space to enhance the natural features. They had brought in large boulders to make small mountains on either side of the river, planted large yet charming groves of aspen and spruce—which were currently decked in Christmas lights—and spread the area with limestone paths and picnic areas flanked by bronzed statues of wildlife.

From our picnic table, I could see the back of the block of stores that held my uncles' antique shop. Only in Estes Park would the backside of shops be nearly as charming as the front. Even the alleyways between some of them looked more like rock-and-brick Tuscan lanes, despite a trash dumpster here and there.

Unwrapping the smaller of the two burgers, the one without cheese, I tore it in fourths and laid the pieces at Watson's feet. "You more than earned this, buddy. Diet or not." He'd given me the complete cold shoulder since we left Paws, and as he turned his suddenly happy gaze on me, it looked like I was on my way back to redemption. Although I knew him well enough to be certain one burger wasn't going to cut it. And despite feeling like he understood most of what I said, I hoped he hadn't caught the scheduled playdate. If he had, the next couple of days were going to be full of attitude that no amount of burgers could squash.

Despite the soft clouds covering the sky, the day was bright, and snow drifted lazily. It was cold, but with my down jacket, not uncomfortable. I supposed it would have been smarter to eat inside the bookshop, but after Paulie, I felt the need for fresh air. And I definitely owed it to Watson.

The tourists doing their Christmas shopping were fewer on the backside of the stores, and with the winding paths and semiforested areas, I almost felt secluded in our little Christmas scene.

By the time I was halfway through my cheeseburger and fries, I was nearly human again. Which made me think of Katie. The next stop would be to her. Maybe I would take her a cheeseburger. Though if I remembered Branson's schedule correctly, he was supposed to be back tomorrow. Surely he would get Katie out, since I had little hope her incompetent lawyer could.

Maybe my next stop should be going back home to my computer and searching out lawyers in Denver.

Between the snow, branches of leafless aspens, and my thoughts, I almost missed the movement in the alley several yards away behind the shops. But when I recognized Daphne's beautiful raven hair flowing down her back, I zeroed in on her. She tossed a large bag into the dumpster and then stood, her hands covering her face. Her shoulders shook so that even from a distance it was easy to see she was crying.

My suspicions about her once again made me feel guilty. I'd wondered if she'd tried to kill her husband, and here she was, sobbing. Despite how horrible Declan seemed to be, apparently she loved him. As I considered whether I should go over and offer to comfort her, or move away to give her privacy, she was joined by someone else. Dolan's hair made him just as recognizable as Daphne. His coppery orange coloring nearly glowed through the falling snow.

Proving that he had a gentle soul like I'd heard, he wrapped Daphne in his arms, comforting her. At least she had Declan's family for support. What it must be like to be expecting your first child and not sure where your husband's coma would leave you.... Poor woman.

Just as I was about to turn away, Dolan broke their embrace, pulling back slightly, as he said something to his sister-in-law. And then he kissed her. I jolted from my spot on the picnic bench, causing

Watson to startle as well. I instantly began to explain away the kiss. Just a simple sign of affection between family. I myself had kissed my uncle on the lips that very morning. But then Daphne ran a hand up Dolan's back and her fingers stroked through his hair, pulling him toward her, deepening the kiss.

Maybe not the concerned wife after all....

SEVEN

"Katie, we really don't have to do this." I grinned at her over the stack of books, three boxes high, between us. "It's your first day as a free woman. Surely there are more fun things you'd rather do."

She shook her head, curls flying. "No. It feels good to help." She bent, chose a few books from a box, and started arranging them on the shelf. "I got to sleep in this morning, in my own bed, praise the Lord! That's all I really wanted."

"Didn't like the cots in the jail, huh? If I remember correctly, Barry thought they were the height of luxury."

She cringed, then cocked her brow. "Nothing against Barry, but you have met your stepfather, correct?"

I chuckled and shelved some more books for my side of the room. While I was a control freak, when Katie suggested helping with inventory, I couldn't turn her down. We were starting in the main room, though. I was going to keep the mystery room for myself.

"Speaking of elderly white guys, did you call the one I found for you down in Denver? I was so mad I could have strangled Officer Green last night when she wouldn't let me visit you, but it did give me time to research decent lawyers."

Katie hesitated and then shrugged. "No, I didn't. I don't think I need to go down that road. At least Sergeant Wexler made it seem like Officer Green had been an idiot to suspect me. I really think it's over. And I'm saving up to try to get a spot for my bakery, as you know. The last thing I want to spend a small fortune on is a lawyer. After all, there are two empty shops beside you. Maybe one of them will end up being mine."

I'd known it had been Katie's hope. Unfortunately the property had been left to some of Lois and Opal's long-lost family in Oklahoma, who were now squabbling about what to do with their inheritance, so the stores sat vacant.

As I spoke, I kept my attention firmly away from Katie. "I'm so glad that Bran—Sergeant Wexler showed up last night and got you out of jail. I didn't think he was coming back until today."

"Well, it was nearly one in the morning, so technically...." I could feel Katie's gaze on me. "Haven't heard from him yet?"

I shook my head. "No. No reason that I should."

"Right." She snorted. "No need to pretend with me, remember? Nor for you to call him *Sergeant Wexler*."

I cast her a glare.

Katie merely shrugged again. "What? It's true. And let me tell you, he was a real knight in shining armor last night. The way he came storming in there. I had the impression he had barely gotten back to Estes and came directly to the station when he heard about me." Katie's tone was heavy with innuendo. "And we both know he didn't do that for me."

"Of course he did. He's a good police officer. Anyone who knows you knows you couldn't kill someone."

"Sergeant Wexler doesn't really know me, as you are aware, Fred."

"Maybe so, but he's not an idiot. As if in those three minutes it took me to catch up with you at the toy store you went in, entered some state of rage, and attempted to kill a man twice your size, only to have me walk in and you switch courses." Despite my protestations, the thought that I'd been the reason

Branson had hurried down to the police station in the middle of the night made my heart do things that simply annoyed me. "It didn't have anything to do with me."

Katie gave another snort but didn't press the issue. She shelved a few more books, and then her tone switched from teasing to irritation. "I didn't tell you. Guess who gave me a good talking-to as soon as I woke up."

I turned to her. "I have no idea. Who?"

"Carla!" Katie bugged her brown eyes at me. "Can you believe it? She said she heard that I got out of jail and wanted to know why I hadn't shown up for my shift this morning."

I nearly laughed, then realized Katie wasn't joking. "You're serious?"

Katie nodded. "Dead serious. And I thought Opal had been a hard boss."

Maybe I'd have to reconsider and start driving the farther distance to get my coffee across town. "You deserve better than that. I sure hope things get cleared away with the stores next door. It would be so wonderful to have you as a neighbor, and you living your dream as a baker. Wouldn't that be perfect? Me in my dream bookshop and you in your dream bakery?"

She paused, giving me a strange look, and when she spoke, her voice was hesitant. "Actually, about that... I've been thinking—"

She was interrupted by a knock at the door. We both turned, and my heart skipped a beat, betraying me utterly.

"Well, speak of the devil. A handsome devil."

I ignored Katie's jibe, took a breath, and headed over to unlock the door and let Sergeant Wexler in. It'd been a couple of weeks since I'd seen him.

He smiled at me warmly, and for a second, I thought he was going to give me a hug. Probably would've if I hadn't stiffened. "You're a sight for sore eyes, Fred."

Was I? "Oh please, you just returned from a two-week vacation. I'm sure I can't compare to whatever sundrenched beach you were on."

He twisted his lips. "I wouldn't exactly call it a vacation." He stepped the rest of the way in, so I could close the door, and shot another smile at Katie. "Heard you broke out of the big house last night."

"Thanks to you." Katie's smile was easy, and though she found him handsome, it was clear he didn't have the same effect on her as he did on me. "Thanks for coming to my rescue, Sergeant."

He let out an annoyed sigh. "Don't thank me for

that. You shouldn't have been there to begin with. Just sorry I wasn't here when you two needed me." Those green eyes flashed toward me again. "Can I help unbox some books?"

Like he had once or twice before, his offer only served to discombobulate me. The men in my family, my father and uncles, Barry, and even my step-brother-in-laws, were always gentlemanly and kind where their wives and female relatives were concerned. And even though I'd been divorced for many years, I somehow expected to be treated like a servant by any man who wasn't part of my family. I was constantly on guard against it, truth be told.

"That would be great. Thank you. But aren't you on duty? I don't know how the city would feel about their tax dollars for your salary going to getting the Cozy Corgi ready."

With a wink, he walked over to the box Katie was emptying and joined her. "Well, I can multitask. I'm not just here to unbox inventory. I'm here on official police business." He shrugged. "Well, sort of unofficial police business."

Katie straightened. "Please don't tell me you have to take me back in. Even for questioning. If I never see the inside of another police station, it will be too soon."

Chuckling, he patted her shoulder and shook his head. "No. You're good. Although—" He glanced back at me. "—as ludicrous as the situation was to consider Katie a real suspect, I can't completely blame Officer Green for what she did. Did you know the only fingerprints found on that hideous nutcracker were Katie's and the members of the Diamond family? I'm not saying Katie would do such a thing, especially with you being mere moments behind her, but one would expect there to be other fingerprints, don't you think?"

"You did say you found fingerprints of some of the other members of Declan's family. Maybe one of them...." All of a sudden it hit me. Branson had come here, to us, to me. And was discussing facts of the case which he most definitely shouldn't be. "Wait a minute. What's going on here? Why are you telling us this?"

He shelved another book and then turned fully toward me, the emotion in his eyes unnameable. Or at least something I was uncomfortable naming. "We may not know each other all that well, Winifred Page, but I'd bet my badge that the moment your friend was accused of attempted murder, you took matters into your own hands."

I hesitated, trying to determine if I was getting

set up. "You made it very clear, Sergeant Wexler, that I was to keep my nose in my own business. Leave the police work to the police, if I recall."

He smirked, the expression somehow making him even more dashing. "And I seem to remember you telling me you don't like being told what to do. And that if you got it in your mind, you could probably solve a case quicker than any of us."

"I don't know if those were my exact words."

Another smirk. "So you want me to pretend you haven't been going around asking questions?"

I wasn't sure how to answer him. I knew my uncles hadn't called to complain. And I was highly doubtful Paulie would either. And I hadn't gotten a chance to ask anyone else. After I'd been turned away from seeing Katie, I'd spent the rest of the evening finding a decent lawyer for her. That had seemed more vital at the moment. "Nobody's called you. You're just guessing."

"I wouldn't call it guessing. I think I've got your number."

"Now you listen here." Katie's voice rose in temper as she rounded on Branson. "Anything Fred might have done, and I'm not saying she's done anything, was to help me. You've pretty much said yourself that the police were making a mistake by arresting me. What do you expect—"

"Whoa, whoa." He held up his hands in surrender. "Number one, I wasn't complaining." He glanced my way again. "And you've already proven to me you have a quick brain and you're a natural. As long as you're not breaking any laws or intentionally hampering a police investigation, I'm not about to stand in your way."

I balked, completely thrown off guard. "You're not?"

Branson smiled, almost gently. "Should I? Is it what you expect, for me to tell you that since you're not a police officer you don't know what you're doing? Or that just because your father was a detective doesn't mean you inherited his innate skill? Or do you expect me to simply tell you to leave it to the big boys? That it's man's work?"

Yes, to all of it. It was exactly what I'd expected. And though I didn't say so, I knew my answer was clear in my eyes.

He studied me for a moment. And while it made my cheeks heat, it wasn't an entirely unpleasant experience. Finally, with Katie glancing back and forth between the two of us, he continued as if nothing had been said. "If you have any information that would help, I'd appreciate it. Like I said, it was ludicrous to think Katie had anything to do with this, given the circumstances, but I can't entirely blame Officer Green —as much as I might like to—given the fingerprints."

Okay, it looked like we were actually going to do this. I swallowed and then began. "You said there were other prints on the nutcracker, those belonging to Declan's family. Maybe it was one of them."

He tilted his head, and I could tell from his expression it wasn't a revelatory thought to him. The corner of his lip turned into a grin. "Very true. But the problem is, the other problem, there were only two types of blood present at the scene. Declan's and Katie's. If another member of his family had tried to kill him with that garland, their blood would be there too."

"Well, I hadn't thought of that." Katie glanced at her hands, which she'd mentioned were still tender. "There's no way anybody could wrap that garland around his neck and not get cut themselves."

That answer was obvious. "Unless they wore—"

"Hello! Hope I'm not intruding."

I turned toward the voice, and for a moment didn't recognize the woman standing in the doorway. I guess I'd forgotten to lock the door after letting

Branson in. The blonde's smile faltered when she noticed Branson and Katie.

"Sorry. I guess I'm intruding. I just needed a break from the shop and thought I'd talk to you about the logo. But I can come back."

And with that, it clicked—the woman from Rocky Mountain Imprints. "Peg. I'm so sorry. In all of the chaos, I'd forgotten all about the Cozy Corgi logo." I turned to Branson and then Katie. "You remember me mentioning that right? Maybe turning the second floor into Cozy Corgi merchandise."

Katie's grimace surprised me, but it turned to a quick smile. "Yes, I do."

"Sounds like a good idea." Branson nodded toward Peg. "Nice to see you, Peg. Everything going well with you and Joe?"

She nodded. "Of course."

"Good. I'll actually be stopping by later this morning. I know you two already gave statements to the police, but since you're right next door and I'm playing catch up, it would be great if I could have a moment of your time. You never know when someone might know something, even if they're not aware of it."

"Sure." Peg shifted a few pieces of paper to her other hand, different products that would be used for the logo, I assumed. "Whenever you want to come down, Sergeant, Joe and I will be ready for you. You're always welcome."

It suddenly felt like four was a crowd. "Peg, do you mind showing the sketches to Katie? Let me finish up with Brans... er... Sergeant Wexler?"

Peg was just as tiny as a pixie, like she'd been before, and just as quick. Her eyes widened at my slip. She cast a quick glance toward Branson. I needed to be more careful. I didn't know Peg, but if she was even half the gossip as my uncles, there would be more fun rumors flying around town by the afternoon.

"Oh, of course. Plus, it looks like you got your hands full here. I have a strong husband back at the shop that I can loan you for a few hours this afternoon if you need to expedite getting all the books unpacked."

Branson snorted. "You're the one who earned all those trophies for the softball team, not Joe."

Pride sparkled in her eyes. "True, but he can bench-press more, so he gets to do all the heavy lifting." Peg refocused on me. "He really wouldn't mind helping."

"Thank you, that's very kind, but I wouldn't dream of imposing." I glanced at Katie. I wasn't sure why she seemed not to like the idea of the corgi merchandise, but I hoped whatever sketches Peg had would change her mind. Likewise, I wasn't entirely certain why Katie's opinion on the issue mattered all that much. I wasn't in the market for a new business partner. "See what you think about them, Katie. Let me finish up with Sergeant Wexler, and I'll be right over."

Reminding myself that not only was I not looking for a new business partner, but neither was I looking for a man. It was easy to forget that while in Branson Wexler's presence. We took a few paces away, and I lowered my voice. "As I was saying, you're right about the blood and that garland, but the attacker could have been wearing gloves, couldn't they?"

"Of course they could've." He grinned. "See, I knew you had instinct."

Though I could tell he was being kind and flattering me, I couldn't keep from rolling my eyes. "Oh, come on, now. Don't be insulting. It doesn't take much instinct to know that if the prints you're looking for aren't there, gloves are probably involved." I cast a glance around him, making sure Peg wasn't listening. Having her potentially gossip about Branson and I would be one thing. Running back to tell her business neighbor that I was accusing them of trying to kill a member of their family was an entirely different one. "But maybe the attacker was a member of Declan's own family. Watson and I"—I motioned upstairs as if Watson's current location mattered in the moment—"saw Dolan and Daphne kissing this afternoon. And not a brother and sister-in-law kind of kiss, if such a thing even exists."

"Really?" His eyes widened, and any level of flirting that had been there left his tone. "Now that is news." He considered for a moment. "That would for sure point to possible suspects. Daphne trying to get out of her marriage, and Dolan in a fit of jealous brotherly rage." Branson squinted at another thought. "Although I just can't see Daphne being able to do that kind of damage. Declan is a big man."

"That's what I was thinking. Although everyone talks about how wonderful and kind Dolan is."

Branson didn't seem concerned by the thought. "He wouldn't be the first one who's tried to kill for his brother's wife." He shrugged again. Then his tone lightened. "Maybe it will all be a moot point soon anyway. From what I hear, Declan's situation is improving. With a coma, there's never really any guarantee of when the person might wake up, but if and when he does, chances are he'll know who his attacker was. Unless it was a complete surprise, since the impact came from behind. The doctor is hopeful he'll wake soon."

Katie let out a relieved sigh. I hadn't noticed the two of them coming closer to us. "Well, that's wonderful news. I'm ready for this to be behind me." She blushed. "And for Declan to be okay, of course."

Branson chuckled. "I can see why you two get along so well." He gave a quick nod toward Peg but kept his eyes on me. "I know you've got things to talk about. But you and I discussed some things before I left town. I believe Christmas was the deadline, correct?" He gave a wink and a pretend tilt of the hat that wasn't there and strode to the door before turning around and offering a model-perfect smile. "Ladies." And then he was gone.

Try as I might, I couldn't really focus as I looked at the printouts of different merchandise with the Cozy Corgi logo on them that Peg offered. My thoughts instead swirling around Branson still wanting to go out to dinner. To go on a date.

It was so much more stressful than trying to figure out what to put on the second level of my shop or who had attempted to kill Declan Diamond.

EIGHT

"The hoodies with the Cozy Corgi logo on them were really great. The hats were good too." I'd ordered a hoodie from Peg before she left, just to see, and now I studied Katie's expression as she firmly kept her attention on arranging the books. "I thought the shot glasses were a bit too much, though. I'm not sure it's quite the branding I want to go with."

Katie let out a puff of air but gave no further commentary, just reached for another book.

I couldn't say that Katie seemed angry after Peg left, but she wasn't her normal self either. "Do you know something about Peg that I don't?"

She looked at me wide-eyed, startled. "No. I don't think so. Why?"

"It just seems that every time I bring it up, you seem a bit uncomfortable. I thought maybe Peg was another Opal or Carla-type person."

"No, I don't think so." She smiled, but it was

clearly forced, as was the ease in her tone. "And yes, the hoodie was adorable, the hats were indeed great, and totally a big fat no on the shot glasses."

Whatever tension was suddenly between us was one more confirmation about me needing to do this on my own. "Well, I'm glad we agree, then."

Katie shelved another couple of books, then turned to get a better look at me from across the room.

"It's just that I was thinking maybe we could—" Her gaze flicked over my shoulder, out the window, and she flinched. "What in the world?"

I turned around to see what she'd noticed. It only took me a second, and I choked back a laugh. Directly across the street, in the store Cabin and Hearth, Anna and Carl Hanson were openly gaping at Katie and me through their window. Maybe there was a glare, as Anna had both her hands pressed to the glass over her brow. As soon as they noticed me looking back, they both gave a little jump, waved awkwardly, and trundled away. I angled back to Katie, chuckling. "They're not exactly subtle, are they?"

"You think?" She grinned, the tension from before fading. "I know I'm no super sleuth, but my keen intuition is telling me they might want to talk to you."

I considered for half a second. Branson had pretty much said Katie was cleared, mostly, despite the fingerprints, considering she had me as an alibi, so I couldn't pretend I was doing this for Katie. I'd simply be doing it because I was curious, because I wanted to figure it out. There would be nothing altruistic about it from this point onward.

I was okay with that.

I put the book I'd been holding on the shelf and dusted my hands on my skirt—more habit than anything, since the new books didn't have a lick of dust on them. "Do you mind if I go chat with them? As you can see, very little that happens in town gets past them."

Again Katie's grin was genuine. "I'd expect nothing less. And I look forward to hearing what you find out."

"Well then, be right back." I walked over to the counter and grabbed my purse, slung it over my shoulder, and began to head for the door, then remembered Anna's affinity for dogs. Stopping at the base of the steps, I hollered up to the second floor. "Watson! Nap time's over."

A second or two passed, and then a loud yawn

made its way downstairs. I could just picture him, stretching out his front paws with his knob-tailed rump sticking in the air. A few more seconds passed, and then the slow padding of his paws sounded over the hardwood.

Katie joined me. "He really likes to take his time, doesn't he?"

That was an understatement. "Just reminding me who's in charge."

"Apparently."

"Want to see the tables turn?" I gave her a wink, and she nodded. I refocused upstairs and raised my voice once more. "Watson, treat!"

The clattering of his paws went from church mouse to herd of elephants in a heartbeat. From our vantage point, Katie and I could see him rush around the edge of the banister, lose his traction on the newly refurbished hardwood floors, his hind legs skidding out from behind him. He managed to catch himself before crashing into the wall, and then tore down the steps, eyes wild with excitement and tongue whipping like a flag from his mouth. He came to a skidding stop at my feet, this time not quite managing on the slick floor, and bumped into my ankles.

Katie nearly doubled over in laughter.

Watson didn't spare her a glance, his gaze traveling from both my hands up to my face, clearly asking what the trick had been.

I tickled the pink spot on his muzzle. "You're an embarrassment to corgis everywhere, sir."

He glowered, whined, and then gave a tentative hop on his front paws, reminding me of the magic word I'd uttered.

"Come with me. We're heading over to see Anna. She has your treat."

Watson piped up again at the word and followed me without argument as we left the shop, crossed the street, and walked into Cabin and Hearth.

The home décor shop was like stepping into a high-end log cabin. Though the place was crowded with merchandise, it oozed comfort, charm, and coziness. But at the same time, it only took a glance to know that every piece would cost a small fortune.

Anna and Carl were standing behind the counter, both furiously studying some paperwork they held between them. If I hadn't known they were there, I might not have recognized them. They were both short and round, Anna with white poufy hair, while Carl was bald and wore glasses. I guessed them both to be in their sixties. The first time I met them, they reminded me of Mr. and Mrs. Claus, but now, they *were* Mr. and Mrs. Claus. Complete with fuzzy red outfits lined in white fur, Carl's cinched by a large glistening black belt straining over his expansive middle, and Anna wearing a frilly reindeer-patterned apron.

I nearly chuckled. They might be grade A gossips, but convincing, they weren't. I decided to play along and not mention the incident at the window, since apparently I was supposed to believe they'd been standing there studying that piece of paper for hours. "Don't you two look simply amazing? I feel like I've just traveled to the North Pole."

The Mrs. Claus version of Anna looked up and played her part so well that she gave a little flinch in surprise. "Oh, Fred, my dear. So nice to see you." The smile she gave me was friendly enough, but it transformed to a thing of genuine beauty when she glanced down at my feet and let out a shrill squeak. "Oh, and Watson!" She smacked Carl on the arm before she hurried around the counter. "Go get him a treat. And put on your beard. How are you going to be Santa without a beard?"

A pink hue rose to Carl's cheeks as he gave me a nod and waddled toward the back room.

Anna reached us in a matter of moments and was on her knees in front of Watson, the red fabric of her skirt billowing out around them. "You just hold on, you little doll. He'll be right back. You'll get your snack."

Watson didn't go hog wild over her like he did for Barry, but whether he actually liked her or considered her a dog treat dispenser, Watson allowed himself to be petted, going so far as to lick her hand.

I was forgotten for the minute or so it took Carl to return. He held out a small brown dog biscuit, which Watson scrutinized for a second, clearly not what he'd expected, but he took it nonetheless.

Anna stood and smacked Carl again, this time audibly. "What is wrong with you? I told you we were saving the dog bones for *Watson*. And you know I give the treats to the dogs, not you." She smacked him again, this time harder. "And you forgot your beard. Again."

His blush deepening, Carl let out an apologetic sigh and left us once more.

Anna shook her head at me, clearly commiserating about how stupid husbands could be. "We only have five of Lois's dog bones left. And I told Carl we were saving every single one for when you and Watson visit. I don't know what we'll do when they're gone, but we'll figure out something."

There'd only been two things Lois Garble had made that anyone liked in her all-natural candy store. One was her hard licorice candy. And the other her all-natural dog bones. In truth, I was a little taken aback. I assumed Anna was like that with every dog, and maybe she was to a degree, but it warmed me a little that she thought so highly of Watson. "That is so sweet of you, Anna."

She waved me off, bending to scratch the top of Watson's head.

Carl was back, large all-natural dog bone in his hand, and a massive Santa Claus beard covering half his face. This time, he remembered protocol, handing the dog bone to Anna so she could in turn offer it to Watson. For his part, Watson was in heaven.

Carl's beard would put Paulie's to shame. "Goodness. You two truly do look like Mr. and Mrs. Claus. It's amazing."

Anna nodded in agreement. "We wear them every year. On Christmas Eve, we go to the hospital and visit all the kids who are there. It's the highlight of our holidays."

It seemed Anna and Carl were full of surprises, and I had vastly underestimated them. I'd chalked them up as being little more than town gossips, which was true, but I hadn't envisioned such kindness from them.

Before I could think of an appropriate response, Anna started in once more, this time directing her full attention on me. "So, tell us all about it. We heard you were there. In truth, I thought you'd come and talk to us before now, but better late than never." She leaned a bit closer, her voice lowering conspiratorially. "We heard there was blood everywhere. Just everywhere. Of course, I said that sounded like nothing more than hype, but that's what we heard."

"No. There wasn't blood everywhere. There was just some." One of the good things about not actually being a detective was that I didn't have to be overly careful about what information I shared. "There was some due to the garland, but it was mostly contained."

Carl let out a huff, and Anna nodded approvingly. "Those boys came here trying to sell us that garland. I know they're your family, but...." She *tsked* and shook her head. "Who wants garland that you have to wear gloves to hang? Christmas is supposed to be beautiful, not bloody."

I couldn't disagree with her. And since they were the center of the gossip world, I assumed they'd already heard, but I wanted to make certain

Katie was cleared all the way around, even in rumors. "Watson had made a mess on the sidewalk while Katie and I were walking to the toy store, so I went back to get a bag and then met her there." I decided to leave out that I couldn't find one, lest she deem me an unworthy corgi mama and closed up the gossip shop. "It was a matter of a couple of minutes, and I walked in and Katie was kneeling there, struggling to get the garland off Declan's neck, cutting herself in the process. She saved his life."

Anna and Carl had both been nodding through my spiel, clearly having heard it all, but stopped at that last pronouncement. "Katie saved his life?"

"Yes. She loosened it enough for me to cut it off, but it was only thanks to her in those minutes before I arrived that it hadn't finished the job." Again, I had no idea how truthful that part was, but it seemed right. And any benefit I could throw Katie's way seemed smart.

Anna shook her finger at Carl. "See, I told you that girl would never be able to hurt someone like that. Even if she did work for Opal."

Carl's eyes narrowed over his fluffy Santa beard. "Actually, what you said was—"

She smacked him again. "Shut up, Carl." She

turned back to me. "It's clear you and Katie are good friends."

"That's true we are. She's a lot of—"

"It's also clear that you and that handsome Sergeant get along too."

How long had they been staring at us through the windows? Although, I knew there were already rumors about Branson and me. "He's a very good police officer."

Anna nodded and smiled, clearly waiting for me to elaborate. When I didn't, she blinked, looking slightly annoyed. "Well, I have to say, I'm not surprised. Declan Diamond is a handsome fiend, but a fiend nonetheless. And obviously since poor little Katie didn't do it, my money is on Duncan. If I had a child and they did to me what Declan did to him, I'd string him up by Christmas tinsel as well."

"I've told you a hundred times, there's no way Duncan would ever do that." It was the first time I'd heard Carl disagree with Anna. Before, he'd pretended to be uncomfortable with her level of gossip, though he soon got roped in right along with her, but not full-out disagreement. "Duncan is a family man through and through. He'd sooner strangle himself than one of his boys."

Anna shrugged, nonplussed, causing her massive

bosom to heave. "You're entitled to your opinion, Carl. You've been wrong plenty of times before."

He glared. "Well, I think it's terrible to point your fingers at that poor man. Like he hasn't been through enough heartbreak without people in the town he grew up in, has been a vital member of, suddenly accusing him of attempting to kill his own child."

That seemed to be the consensus about Duncan Diamond. But I couldn't help but wonder if it was just another offshoot of the good-old-boys club. If they truly believed Gerald Jackson was a decent lawyer, I wasn't sure how much I could trust their judgment about Duncan, either. But it was clear we weren't going to get anywhere besides a marital squabble if we kept going on that train of thought. I was more curious about what I'd seen the day before.

"I've actually heard quite a bit about Declan having affairs. All the while having a newly pregnant wife at home. If I were her, that would make me pretty angry, wouldn't it you?"

Anna sucked in a shocked breath, and her eyes gleamed in delight. "What? You think Daphne might have done it? Now there's a theory I haven't heard."

Again I thought back to not wanting the Diamonds to hear I'd been gossiping about them, though it was much too late for that now. To keep from confirming or denying, I turned my attention to Watson, who was sprawled happily at our feet, still licking his chops. "That was good, wasn't it, little buddy? It's been a little while since you've had one of those."

He cast a glance at me, clearly annoyed I had interrupted his post dog bone euphoria and letting me know he was fully aware I'd been using him this whole time. I doubted he minded too greatly after having had his favorite treat.

To my surprise, Anna wasn't distracted by Watson for once. "I really must say, that is quite a thought. And quite out of the box. I wouldn't even have considered—"

Anna started sucking in several breaths while snapping her fingers and taking a step back, startling Carl and scaring Watson to take shelter behind my skirt. Anna didn't even notice. She began waving her hands in the air. For a second I feared she might be having a seizure. Then she pointed at me, her tone excited euphoria. "But if you put that together with what happened last night at the Chinese restaurant, that might make perfect sense."

There was a pause, and then Carl sucked in a breath of his own. "Oh! You might be right."

They both looked at me, expecting me to have a similar reaction. When no further comment came, I decided to confess. "I'm sorry. I'm not sure what happened at the Chinese restaurant last night. I was at home looking for a good lawyer for Katie, just in case. And then came directly to my shop this morning."

Carl flinched. "A new lawyer for Katie? Why in the world would she need one? Gerald told me he was on her case."

Anna gave one of the largest eye rolls I'd ever seen and stared at her husband like he was the biggest moron in the world. And for once, Anna and I were on the same page. But I couldn't let her get distracted by Gerald Jackson.

"What happened at the Chinese restaurant last night?"

Anna turned back to me, her gaze increasingly hungry as she grew voracious. "Declan served Daphne with divorce papers last night, right in the middle of the Chinese restaurant, right in the middle of everyone having their dinners. Can you imagine how devastating it must be?"

I waited for the punch line, but none came. "I'm sorry, I don't see how that was possible. Declan's in the hospital." When there was still no response, I added for good measure, "In a coma."

This time Anna's eye roll was directed at me. "Well, of course I don't mean Declan himself, dear. But someone on his behalf. He obviously must have arranged for the divorce papers to be delivered before he was attacked two nights ago. It doesn't matter whether or not he's in a coma. I'm sure whoever he hired to do it either didn't know that he had been attacked or had already been paid so figured he should follow through on the job."

That made sense. Kinda. Daphne had gotten her divorce papers last night. One night after Declan was attacked. And just a few short hours after I'd seen her and Dolan kissing. Maybe they had known it was coming.

"Were you there? Did she seem shocked?"

Anna wrinkled her nose while shaking her head. "Goodness no. We only eat American food. Carl's stomach can't handle anything exotic." She actually reached over and patted his extended belly. "But from what I hear, she sat there stone-cold sober and white as a ghost. Hardly any reaction at all, really. Then she handed it to her brother-in-law. But it was Duncan who lost his temper. Got up from the table, yelling at the poor guy who served the papers.

Screaming about how he couldn't do this to their family when they were in the middle of so much hurt." She raised her eyebrows. "Another piece of evidence against Duncan, if you ask me. Losing his temper like that. Right in the middle of a restaurant, in public."

"I'm telling you, Duncan would never be able to do anything like that. He didn't hurt his son."

No, but maybe Declan's brother would. Maybe Declan had found out about their affair and was getting ready to expose it to the rest of the town, or to their father. Or maybe Declan told Daphne he wanted a divorce, and she didn't want to be cut out of the business or the money. Either way, it seemed even from his unconscious state in a hospital room, Declan Diamond was able to cause drama and more pain for his family.

As I left Cabin and Hearth, my mind mulled over all the different possibilities that could have happened within the Diamond family, including that maybe trying to figure out which one of them had tried to kill Declan was a waste of time. Maybe it had been all three. But I thought Katie had said she'd only heard one set of footsteps running away. I'd have to check.

I was so caught up in the speculation that I'd barely taken three steps from their shop when I crashed into someone.

They gave a loud *oof*, and there was a crash of packages to the ground. Watson's barking went wild.

"Oh, I'm so sorry. That was completely my fault. I wasn't watching where I—" My sight caught up to my lips and caused them to close. Or at least quit making words. I was fairly certain my lips were hanging open.

Leo Lopez stretched out a hand to steady me. "Not at all. I'm sure the fault was mine."

His yellow-brown eyes gazed directly into mine for a second, and then he looked down at Watson.

It was only then I realized Watson's frantic barking wasn't due to the collision but to his excitement. He was on his hind legs, his front paws bashing against Leo's knees. Though we'd only met once before, Watson's reaction to Leo had been the same then, like he was another incarnation of Barry.

Leo bent down to ruffle behind Watson's ears with both his hands. "It's good to see you too, little man. You're a good boy. Good boy." Though his tone had slipped slightly into baby talk, it altered to just a touch of heat, though his eyes didn't look up at me. "You've been doing a good job of keeping your mama safe?"

I forced a laugh I hoped sounded natural. "If by safe you mean eating me out of house and home, then yes. Quite safe."

"Good enough, I suppose." Thankfully Leo continued to lavish attention on Watson, allowing me some much needed time to pull myself together.

I'd moved to Estes Park to restart my life. Be with my family, open a cute little bookshop, and read by the fire every night with Watson at my feet. That was it. I was done with romance, done with men, and done with husbands or relationships. It had been bad enough when I'd met Branson Wexler, with all his classic good looks and muscles poured into a police uniform. To make matters worse, I'd run into Leo Lopez a couple of days later. Another man in uniform, this one a park ranger, and with a face and body nearly the carbon copy of a young Oscar De La Hoya—and at five years my junior, I truly meant young. Having only seen him once, I'd managed to put Leo out of my mind—mostly. Judging from the racing of my pulse, my heart couldn't make the same claim.

With Watson's frantic exuberance abated to merely whimpering adoration, Leo picked up a couple of packages in a bag on the ground before smiling at me once more. "It's good to see you, Fred. It's been a while."

Whereas Branson was several inches taller than me, Leo was only slightly just, making it where his eyes could look straight into mine. And even in the winter light, they glowed like honey. I had to look away as I motioned across the street toward my shop.

"I've been so busy, with trying to get the Cozy Corgi ready to open by January, and getting my cabin situated, that I haven't had a spare moment."

"I know. That's what you said when you texted."

Despite there being no accusation in his tone, I couldn't help but feel a reproach, whether intended or not. Leo had sent me a message about a week after we met, saying he would love to get dinner sometime. At that point, Opal's murder had just been solved, and Branson had also asked me to dinner. Maybe I'd taken the easy way out by simply texting back that dinner would be lovely, but at the moment life was too busy with the shop. Basically, the equivalent of *I'd love to, but I have to wash my hair*. The guilt I felt with him standing before me was irritating. I was in Estes Park for myself, not for a man. Not a policeman, not a park ranger, not for any uniform a tall, dark, and handsome might put on.

"I really am busy." Once more I motioned across the street as if he might have forgotten where my store was. "Even right now Katie's in there shelving books. I really should be helping her."

"You don't have to explain to me, Fred. You don't owe me anything." Another smile, completely unflappable. "I'm excited to see the Cozy Corgi. Like I said, having a bookstore where a taxidermy shop used to be sure makes me happier. I hated that place." His tone grew serious, and he touched my arm once more, differently this time. The sensation wasn't unpleasant. "I did want to thank you again. It hasn't stopped the poaching, but at least one more poacher is out of business."

"You know I didn't actually kill Sid, right? I simply found the dead owl in the freezer."

He shrugged as if the finer details didn't matter. "Well, thanks to you, it was one more clue, even if Sergeant Wexler says it's not related."

I'd noticed before, though only hinted at in slight tone and vague dismissals, that Branson and Leo had a past. And not a good one. I tried to brush it off. "Well, anything to help." I gestured toward his package-laden arms, adamantly not noticing the bulges of muscles as I did so. "Doing some Christmas shopping?"

"Sure am. I'm heading home tomorrow. I just finished my shift at the park and needed to come down here and wrap up the rest." He gestured with his chin toward the other block. "Luckily I'd already taken care of toys for the nieces and nephews. Otherwise I'd be out of luck today, considering...." His smile faltered, and he blushed. "Sorry. That was a callous thing to say. One I definitely don't mean. I did hear you and Katie were part of the reason Declan is still alive."

Interesting how the version changed depending

on who I was speaking to. It didn't surprise me this was the take Leo would have. "That's true. It seems he's in a coma, but I've heard he's getting better, so maybe he'll wake up soon and all mysteries will be solved."

Leo cocked his handsome head, a slight dimple forming in his left cheek. "Mystery? You diving into this one too? Like the owl?"

For one embarrassingly long moment, I nearly lied, fearing I would look foolish to him. And once more my irritation flared, and once more, at myself, not him. "I am. At first I just wanted to clear Katie, but it looks like that's already happened. And now" —I shrugged, unwilling to sugarcoat—"well, now I just want to know."

His smile didn't dampen nor did his eyes show any humor. Instead he nodded in approval. "You're a fascinating creature, Fred Page."

"No, not hardly. My father was a detective. There were times he'd talk cases over with me. And I was married to another policeman for a while, though he wasn't half the officer my father was. Or half the man, for that matter." At that, his eyes widened, and I wondered if I'd announced about the ex-husband to try and scare him away. "I guess you could just say it's in my blood."

He was distracted momentarily by Watson pushing at his ankles with his head once again, and he leaned down partially to give him more affection, but didn't take his attention off me. "Like I said, fascinating creature. And I would know. I spend my days with fascinating and beautiful creatures."

It was my turn to blush, and for the third time, I motioned to my store. "I should get back. I really am—"

"Busy." He winked, and though there was no humor in his voice, it still lacked any accusal. "You know, I've heard that about you." He seemed to consider, for the first time, a little unsure. "I'm done with my shopping. I'd be happy to help you... and your friend out. It would go faster with another set of hands. And then I could say I knew the Cozy Corgi back when...."

Having Branson Wexler and Leo Lopez in my shop within an hour of each other was probably the quickest way to set the old place aflame. Or maybe that was just me. "No, but thank you. I do appreciate the offer."

Though his tone didn't change, there was clear disappointment in his eyes. One that matched how I was feeling. "Well then, I'll leave you to it. I look forward to the grand opening."

"Me, too. If it ever gets here." I hesitated, looking for a good way to change my mind, one a little less obvious than *wait, don't leave, please come over*. I couldn't find one. "Have a safe trip and a wonderful holiday with your family."

"Thank you. I hope you and yours have a wonderful one as well." Leo started to walk around me and then paused when he was even with my shoulders, which brought those golden eyes of his even closer. "And, Fred? It really was good to see you."

I nodded and swallowed. He was several paces away when I finally found my voice and mumbled that it was good to see him too. But I was certain he couldn't hear. Then it hit me. I didn't even thank him for his referral to his friend who'd built Watson's dog run. That would be a great conversation restarter, and maybe we could work our way back to him helping Katie and me. Gritting my teeth, I refused to act on the impulse.

Watson whined at Leo's departure, and it took every ounce of my willpower to not turn around and watch him walk away. Instead I checked for traffic, and then Watson and I hurried across the street and back into the Cozy Corgi.

I expected Katie to hurry over and demand to

know what I'd found out from Anna and Carl. Instead she leaned against a half-filled bookcase with arms folded and one eyebrow cocked. "Well, Winifred Page, you've been holding out on me. I didn't know you had *two* suitors."

"I don't. I don't even have one...." Why in the world was I bothering to lie about something so completely obvious to everyone? Whatever, I stuck with it. "I'm here for family, books, and hopefully one day homemade baked goods when you open your bakery. Other than that, men are off the table."

Katie unfolded her arms and started to shake her finger at me.

I cut her off. "And what were you doing watching out the window, Little Miss Nosey? You trying to give Anna and Carl a run for their money? I would've thought better of you, Katie Pizzolato."

She rolled her eyes. "Then you'd be wrong." Her smile grew a little more wicked, and her voice held a touch of singsong in it. "But whatever you want to tell yourself, my friend. You are here for the family, books, and baked goods. Right. And I'm here for the way the lack of humidity makes my lips chapped all the time. It's wonderful."

"You know what, you're a—"

Katie cackled and shook her head. "A truly wonderful and adorable individual. I know."

A laugh burst from me. "Well, that much is true, I suppose."

We ordered a pizza and worked for another hour or so, then separated for the evening. It was clear that despite her sleeping in, Katie was still exhausted from her time in jail. Watson and I drove home, past the new developments of mini mansion log cabins, and wound our way through the forest back to what had been my grandparents' old genuine log cabin. We had just stepped inside, me already envisioning curling up by the fire, when another thought hit me.

I hurried to the kitchen and retrieved a small treat from the corgi-shaped cookie jar for Watson, not that he needed another one, but in prepayment for what I knew would annoy him. "I'll be right back. I won't be gone more than an hour."

As he scarfed down the treat, I hurried outside, locked the door, and jumped back into the Mini Cooper. I wasn't sure whether the hospital staff would let me into Declan's room, but I thought I had a good chance. Since it was well-known I was there that night, and even though some were accusing

Katie of trying to kill him, plenty were saying I was the reason Declan was still alive. I couldn't even fully fathom what I expected to find, but something. Even if it was just a gossipy nurse mentioning who had visited or if he'd mumbled something in his coma-induced confusion.

Or, the way my luck was running with hand-some men over the past afternoon, maybe I'd walk into his room and he would wake up. Ask to take me to dinner or some such nonsense. Despite myself, the thought made me chuckle. The man might be a womanizer, and he might've been charming when we'd met, but I highly doubted, at least judging from his wife, that tall, broad, and long auburn-haired was Declan's go-to for dinner dates. But I wouldn't have thought it would be true for Branson and Leo either.

Luckily, as I'd experienced before in the police station, the hospital was also a stereotype of small-town life. There were no guards on duty, no front desk to check in, not even on the neuro unit floor, where I knew he was being held.

I walked, unharassed, down the hallway, checking out names written in dry-erase marker under the room numbers. I heard a door slam, causing me to jump, but no one was coming for me, so I continued on. Halfway down the hall, I found it

—Room 324, D. Diamond. Glancing around once more, I noticed a couple of nurses at the far end of the hall talking to a policeman, probably a guard who was supposed to be at Declan's door. None of them looked my way, so I stepped inside.

Like every other hospital room before it, the space was nondescript, smelling of antiseptic, and even with the solitary string of Christmas lights hung over the shut window, it was depressing in the dim light. The only sound was the beeping of his monitors and the mechanical wheeze of the ventilator. Somehow, despite wires and tubes seeming to pour from his arms, bandages encircling his neck, and his mouth and nose covered with equipment to keep him breathing, surrounded by all the mundane, Declan looked like a male version of Snow White. Simply waiting for a kiss.

Well, good luck, buddy. From what I hear, you've had more than your share of kisses.

I took a couple of steps closer to the bed, still not sure what I was looking for. There were a few cards on the bedside table, a Get Well Soon balloon, and a small potted Christmas tree pruned from a rosemary plant. There was no blue soldier nutcracker, no flashing garland, no killer's gloves. Nothing.

Just Declan.

"Who did this to you?" I narrowed my eyes at him, daring him to wake up and answer. "And what horrible thing that you did caused you to earn it?"

He sucked in a breath, gagged around the ventilator, and I expected his eyes to open as he answered me. The steady beat of the monitor glitched, the pattern continuing in a staccato rhythm and then changed to one long continuous, uninterrupted beep. I glanced at the heart monitor, just in time to see the jagged red spikes trail off into a flat line.

My own heart decided to flip, and then my feet moved even before my brain told me what to do. I rushed to the door and nearly threw myself out into the hallway. "Help! We need a nurse here! Quick!"

Three nurses were already rushing down the hallway, apparently having been alerted by some system. The policeman wasn't with them. They darted past me, not sparing a glance, and gathered around Declan.

I leaned against the outside of the doorframe. Listening. Less than half a minute later, there were more footsteps, and a middle-aged woman in a lab coat also hurried past me and into the room. A doctor, I presumed.

I could barely hear what they were doing over my pounding heart, over my brain screaming at me to leave, to get out of there. But I couldn't; I was frozen. Stillness was what finally forced me to move. When I noticed the steady beep had been silenced, I realize Declan Diamond was dead. For a heartbeat, I considered staying where I was, but then I pictured Officer Green arriving on the scene. It didn't matter if Branson was back in town or not. I glanced around, noticed the stairwell a few doors down, and took the escape offered.

TEN

Even with the snow falling outside my living room window, the sparkling Christmas tree directly in front, the cozy warmth and glow of the fire, the steaming hot chocolate beside the overstuffed armchair, the unread book on my lap, and the softly snoring corgi at my feet, my brain refused to shut down, and my blood seemed incapable of slowing its rapid race through my veins.

I had been in the room the moment Declan Diamond died.

And I'd run.

At least I'd called for help, not that it had done any good. But I'd run.

One second I was stressing over how it would look if one of the nurses recognized me. Dreading Officer Green's reaction to me at the hospital would be nothing compared to her showing up at my door. And the next moment, I was plunged into a crisis of identity. I was Winifred Wendy Page, daughter of Charles Page, the best detective in the entire world, who died in the line of duty. I did not run away. No matter what.

But I had. Maybe I really was just a bookshop owner. Nothing more, nothing less. I supposed that wasn't anything to be ashamed of. But this felt so right, helping Barry, then Katie, then simply trying to put the puzzle pieces together. But this wasn't a puzzle. It was life and death. And as Charles Page's daughter, I should know that better than most.

When the headlights flashed over the living room as a car drove up, then parked in front of the porch, I was almost relieved. At least one of these scenarios would be over—I could quit worrying about whether I was recognized, or stop anticipating the condescending glee in Officer Green's eyes as she took me in for questioning.

It would be done.

Watson leaped up, barking when the knock sounded on the door. I patted his head. "It's okay, boy." Then I stood and walked over to the front door. I nearly just threw it open, but then reminded myself I was a single woman, living alone in a log cabin in the middle of the woods. And it seemed this beautiful tourist trap of a town wasn't quite the safe haven

I'd envisioned. I looked through my recently installed peephole and nearly did a double take. Not Officer Green.

I opened the door. "Hey. What are you doing here?"

Branson stomped snow onto the mat, then stepped inside, looking larger than life in his uniform, complete with bulletproof vest and gun holster. He gave me a sidelong glance. "Do you really need to ask that?"

No, of course I didn't. It was a different person than I'd expected, but the result was the same. "Let me grab my jacket, and I'll come with you."

He gave a little flinch. "Come with me?"

"Yes. Down to the station for questioning."

He studied me for a moment, then shut the door. I'd not even noticed the cold air and snow coming in nor Watson taking a protective stance between us.

"Do you want to go down to the station?"

I considered. Maybe I was reading this wrong. Maybe all my fears had been for nothing. The nurse hadn't recognized me. Why would they, really; I was new in town. Just because a lot of people seemed up on gossip didn't mean everyone was. Maybe Branson was here as a precursor to the dinner he wanted to take me on, though that didn't seem his style. Nor was it something I was comfortable with. But given the circumstances, possibly the better of two options. Well, whatever. I'd been sitting by the fire beating myself up for running away. I didn't care if Branson knew or not. I wanted all my cards on the table. I wanted to feel like Charles Page's daughter again.

"I was at the hospital when Declan Diamond died this evening. I figured that's why you were here."

Branson's lips twitched, and I thought he was going to smile, but he held it back. "Yes. That's why I'm here. I thought I'd have to worm that out of you somehow."

So he had known. "You're not taking me down to the station?"

His brows furrowed, and then he glanced around the cabin. "You've done a lot of work since I was here last. Looks like a real home. It suits you."

"Thanks. It's definitely better. I'm going to replace a few of the things I have now. Start fresh. In fact, I hope—" I realized what we were talking about. "Wait, what are we doing? Why we talking about my house right now?"

Branson shrugged, then the smile did arrive. "Just saying this is a nice place to have a discussion, much better than the police station, don't you think?"

I considered for a moment. "I take it this isn't official?"

Another shrug. "No reason for it to be, I don't think. Unless you had something to do with his death?"

I flinched. "No, of course not. But shouldn't you—"

"Oh, Fred." The smile remained, and Branson shook his head. "I really do have your number. You're a by the book kind of woman. And I'm willing to bet that detective father of yours was a by the book kind of guy as well."

"He was. And I'd like to think that I am."

"Yeah. I can see the condemnation in your eyes. You're actually judging me for *not* taking you down to the station." He gave a little laugh. "I'm not always a by the book kind of guy, Fred. You and I both know you didn't kill Declan Diamond. So why in the world would I bring you down?"

He could see judgment? I hadn't even been aware I felt that. Though, maybe I did. "Well, obviously someone recognized me. Doesn't this need to be on the books in order to be official? Otherwise it will have to happen again."

He sighed, looked around once more, and motioned toward my mug by the armchair. "It's been a long night, Fred. Mind making me a cup of whatever you're having?"

"You want hot chocolate?"

He gave a little eye roll, but his grin grew. "Well, to be honest, I was hoping for something stronger, but sure, hot chocolate sounds great."

I nearly argued for a moment, told him that yes, I did want to go down to the station. Make this official, but maybe he was right. And honestly, I was tired of thinking.

"Fine. Come on. I have a pot simmering on the stove." I turned and headed to the kitchen, Watson at my feet and Branson trailing behind.

He took the same seat at the table he'd sat in the one other time he'd been here as I got a mug out of the cabinet and ladled in hot chocolate.

"I see you truly did decide to keep the tie-dye flamingo curtains, huh?"

They were an eyesore, but were from Barry and my mom. I barely noticed them any longer, and when I did, they brought a smile to my face. "They have character."

"They definitely have something." Branson chuckled as he took the mug from my hands and breathed in the smell of cinnamon and chocolate before letting out a long sigh. "Actually, this is perfect."

I let him have a drink and then decided to push. "So fine, you're not taking me down to the station, but obviously someone recognized me, so fill me in. Why are you talking to me here instead of where you should?"

"You weren't recognized, actually." He smirked a bit. "We'd already taken everyone's reports, and Officer Green was speaking with the doctor, when one of the nurses found me and said she just remembered there'd been a tall kind of redheaded woman who called for help from his room. That in all the chaos she'd forgotten."

"Kind of redheaded woman?" As if that was the point.

"Her words, not mine." He grinned again. "I could go on about the luxurious color of your hair, but I'll save that till after you agree to have dinner with me."

"You're ridiculous." I refilled my own mug of hot chocolate and lifted it to my lips to hide any sort of reaction or blush my body might betray.

"You know, I've heard that before." He set his mug on the table between us. "You weren't technically recognized, but there was only one tall, kind of redheaded woman who would randomly be in Declan Diamond's room around the time he was murdered."

"A fair deduction, I'll give you that. And yes, I was there. I wanted to see if I noticed anything, something that the police missed, or talk to the nurses and see who all came to visit. But—" Branson's words cut through my thoughts. "Did you say murdered?"

He nodded slowly. "So you didn't know that?"

"No. I was barely there any time, but he seemed normal when I walked in, totally fine. All the beeping of the machines was steady. And then they changed all of a sudden, and he flatlined."

Though his green eyes narrowed, I didn't see any distrust there. "You had to have missed the killer by seconds."

"That doesn't even make sense, Branson." I shook my head, trying to think through it. But no one had been there. "There was a policeman talking to some nurses down the hall. He would've noticed."

"He didn't notice you, did he?" He cocked a brow. "Officer Borland isn't the star of the station, let's put it that way."

That much had been obvious. He didn't come running with the nurses. Probably stepped into the restroom or out for a smoke. "Even so, I was in Declan's room. Nothing happened. One minute his heart was beating along just fine, and the next it wasn't."

Branson took another drink, then nodded slowly. "Heart attack. It looks like the lines were tampered with, though. Someone put in a nice little air bubble. Could've done anything. Caused a stroke, respiratory failure, but in Declan's case, a heart attack. Of course, that's all speculation until confirmed by autopsy, but it was clear enough." He leveled his gaze on me, all serious this time. "I know you didn't do it, Fred. I don't want to cause any grief for you or your family after everything that's already happened. If you saw anything, I need to know. Depending on that, we may have to go down to the station and make an official report. But I'll try not to. Do you remember anything?"

"Like I said, Branson, I don't mind being taken down. It's the right thing—"

"I got it, Nancy Drew. You do the right thing. I know." He reached out and covered my hand with his on the tabletop. "Do you remember anything?"

I started to argue but decided it would be pointless. I closed my eyes, picturing the scene. Hearing the beeping of the machines, smelling the disinfectant. I started to shake my head, then heard the pounding of the nurses' feet running toward me, then remembered running away myself, the slam of the door as I booked it down the stairwell and out to my car. My eyes flew open.

"The door."

His eyebrows raised. "The door?"

"Yeah. The door to the stairwell. When I went out, it slammed."

"I don't see—"

"When I got there, before I arrived at Declan's room, I heard a door slam. I didn't think anything about it. But I'm willing to bet it was the exact same door. You're right. I must've just missed the killer."

"That's all you remember?" He let go of my hand and slumped back in the chair.

"It is. But I didn't even remember that to begin with. At least it's proof, well, kinda, that someone else was there."

He shrugged. "True. But not exactly news. Obviously someone was there since they put air in his IV, and obviously, you barely missed them, given the timing. You sure you didn't see anything? A flash of clothing or something, enough to know if it was a man or woman?"

I shook my head again. "No. Nothing. Sorry."

As Branson bit his bottom lip, considering, I tried once more. "We really probably should go down to the station, do this officially. Just in case."

His eyes flashed with just a hint of annoyance. "No. I told you. There's no reason to. It would just cause more paperwork, and then days of Susan foaming at the mouth as she tried to pin this on you. All the while, whoever really did this has more time to get away or cover their tracks. I don't put rules or protocol over results."

He most definitely wasn't the same kind of cop as my dad. It didn't mean he wasn't a good one, just different. And yet, it brought to mind Leo. How he'd had suspicions the taxidermy shop was involved in some of the poaching, and Branson wouldn't give him the time of day. Branson had been wrong on that one, at least it seemed that way.

"I still think—"

Branson stood. "Fred, if you want to go down and make a statement, be my guest." His voice was hard, not unkind, but firmer than I'd heard it. "But I'm not wasting time doing it. Like I said, it would cause more work for all of us. As I told you earlier today, I have faith in your skills. I'd rather you snoop around over the next day or two, trying to find out what really happened, as opposed to trying to convince Susan you weren't the one to give Declan more air than he needed."

I couldn't say I entirely agreed with Branson, but part of me did. Especially the part about being wrapped up in trying to clear my own name for something I didn't do. Something Officer Green most definitely would take it upon herself to prove that I did. Finally, I nodded. "Okay."

He nodded back, only a touch of his warmth returning. "Great. Thanks for the time and the hot chocolate." His expression altered, something flitted across his face that I couldn't name, and when he spoke again, he was himself once more. "Have a good night, Fred. It's always a pleasure to see you." And with that, he left.

Watson was snoring within ten minutes. I'd be lucky to get even two hours of sleep. Not only did I have the revelations about Declan's murder to consider, but my view of Branson was shifting. He definitely wasn't the type of officer my father was, but I couldn't tell if different always meant bad, or if it simply meant different.

As expected, I was exhausted the next day. So much so, I couldn't think clearly enough to even decide who to speak to about Declan. Instead, I opted for continuing to work at the Cozy Corgi. My brain often started to make connections and opened up to new ideas when it was distracted with something else. Plus, the books weren't going to shelve themselves.

By midafternoon, Katie had finished her shift at the Black Bear Roaster and joined me. I filled her in on the night's events. To my surprise, the only thing she reprimanded me for was not taking her along to the hospital.

Katie's theory was that it was a joint effort between Dolan and Daphne to get the controlling brother and cheating husband out of the way. It was just as good a theory as any. "But just think what that would mean for poor Duncan. His oldest son murdered, his youngest son and daughter-in-law murderers and in jail. And him all alone in that toy shop just whittling away." Katie considered for a moment. "Although Daphne is pregnant, so maybe he could raise his grandchild. But he seems too old and grumpy to do that very well."

Somehow I hadn't even thought about the baby. What a tragedy it would be born into, especially if Katie's theory was correct. "I don't know, I still think Duncan might be responsible. After all the betrayal

Declan put him through. I know everyone says he's got a gentle soul and is just a kind old man, but they also say Gerald Jackson is a fine lawyer, so I'm not keen to put too much stock in Duncan's peers' opinion of him."

As I'd shelved books that morning, it was Duncan I kept returning to. I even walked down to the toy store at lunch, thinking I'd go and buy something, see if I could turn the conversation in a way that might give an idea of what they were feeling. "The toy shop is still closed. And I don't have a good reason to show up on their doorstep. But it really did sound like Declan serving Daphne with divorce papers was the last straw for Duncan. Maybe it's what pushed him to go to the hospital and finish what he'd started."

Katie shook her head but didn't look over at me as she used a box cutter to slice through the tape on a new box of books. "I just don't see it. Duncan, grumpy as he may be, is an artist, a creator. He makes toys for children, for crying out loud. You might as well accuse Santa of being a murderer."

"I don't know if I would go so far as to equate Duncan to Santa. You said yourself, he's grumpy. Santa is supposed to be jolly. As much as I hate to admit it, Carl Hanson makes a much better Santa than Duncan Diamond ever would."

She waved off that thought. "Again, Duncan is a creator. He brings things into the world, not takes them away. Even if his creation was used to try and kill his son." Katie shuddered. "I've never liked those nutcrackers. Even less now."

"They are rather creepy, the way their mouths hang open like that. Just waiting to smash something."

"Did you know—" Katie paused and looked over at me, all seriousness. "—that the first wooden soldier nutcrackers were carved by German miners? It was their side job. They would whittle during their free time and sell them on the side."

"You know, Katie, I definitely can't say I knew that."

She nodded emphatically, sending her curls bobbing in a way that had already grown familiar and endearing. "It's true. And they were often given to German children for good luck."

I gaped at her. "For something that creeps you out as much as you claim, you sure know a lot about them."

She raised a finger. "My favorite fact is that some of them were carved to look like politicians who were despised during the day, and weren't really for cracking nuts at all. Of course the people who made them said any resemblance was completely coincidental, but I do think it explains why I feel the way I do. They're meant to be creepy."

"Katie, what in the world...?" And then it hit me, and I burst into laughter. I'd forgotten about one of her quirks she'd told me about. "Oh, I get it! You got sucked into the never-ending hole of facts and trivia about nutcrackers, didn't you?"

She lifted her chin primly. "Possibly."

She really was something. "I don't think Google is your friend. I'm afraid you might dive in and never come back."

"You have your ways, and I have mine. You might think you can solve a murder by talking to all the big gossips in town, but I happen to think research could shed the most light on things." She flinched a little, though I hadn't said or reacted in any way, and then her tone changed, almost wary, but some other emotion was there as well. Maybe... hope? "It's a different topic, but you want to hear what else I researched?"

From the sound of her voice, I nearly said no, afraid of what was coming. "I bet you're going to tell me."

"Well...." Katie took a shaky breath and then turned away from me, focusing on the books once more. "There's lots of studies saying that bookstores are more successful when there's a bakery up top. Something about the smells of fresh bread and cookies and things making customers below buy more."

The change in topic completely threw me off. "What?"

Still she didn't look at me. Her fingers trembled as she retrieved another book. "It's true. I also read that it's considered good fortune to have bookstores and bakeries together." She cleared her throat. "Something about... the alliteration, I believe. Bookstores and bakeries. B and B. You know, for, um, good luck or something...."

And it clicked. The moment it did, I was nearly ashamed it hadn't clicked weeks before. All the hints she'd dropped, even the irritation Katie always showed when I brought up Peg and turning the second floor into Cozy Corgi merchandise. "Katie?"

"Hmm?" She turned toward me, all wide-eyed innocence, but then looked away again quickly.

"Are you wanting to open your bakery upstairs?"

There was a long pause. She seemed to consider, and then she sucked in her breath. "Well, what a thought? Well, I just don't know... is it something you would want?"

It was so ridiculous, and Katie was more nervous than I'd ever seen her, and I couldn't keep from laughing. I walked over to her, gripped both of her shoulders, and turned her to face me. "How long have you been thinking about this?"

"I don't know." She shrugged unable to meet my gaze for more than a moment, then looking away. "Ever since you found Opal. I mean there's already a kitchen up there. It seems to make sense." She grimaced. "I know that makes me awful. I shouldn't have been thinking about such things when Opal had just been killed. But I've wanted this for so long. And it just seems so utterly perfect. You and I get along.... We have a lot of fun together. It could be this great adventure...."

"Katie. I...." It was so out of the blue. A bakery upstairs. In my bookshop. Another business partner.

She pulled away, and though she sounded disappointed and possibly hurt, she didn't sound angry. "Never mind. I know that's not why you're here. You came up to have your own adventure. To be Winifred and Watson. Just the two of you. I don't want to intrude."

I started to speak, to agree, and then to argue, but

then the picture started to form. She was right. I had come up here to have my own adventure. To finally make life on my own terms. But I hadn't been sure what to do with upstairs. I'd wanted the bookstore to be small and cozy, not some large rambling houseful. I didn't want to rent it out as an apartment either. But a bakery? Katie had a point. It would make the bookshop smell wonderful. It would be a great business to have together. People would come in for pastries and leave with the book, or they'd come in to buy a book, and then they'd wander upstairs to read it over coffee and cake.

It felt right. Scary, but right.

Branson had been correct. I'd always been a by the book kind of woman. In everything. In my studies, my time as a professor, in my marriage, and starting the publishing house with Charlotte. Until everything hit the fan and I decided to hit Reset and throw caution to the wind. That hadn't been by the book. None of this was by the book. And yet I felt like it was working. Bookstore and bakery. What a perfect combination.

I sighed and sank back against the bookshelf. "You're going to make me gain a thousand pounds, aren't you?" I met Katie's gaze as she looked over at me in surprise. "Just remember, there's already been one dead body up in that kitchen. There can easily be another."

"You mean...?" Katie's eyes widened and her expression shifted from disappointment, to confusion, to awe. "You mean...?"

I laughed and felt a giddy sort of thrill course through me. "I mean, Katie, would you consider opening a bakery in the top part of my bookstore? I've heard studies saying that the smell of baked goods can greatly increase the sale of books."

Katie froze, then jumped up and down, and then jogged in place as she squealed. "Yes! Oh, yes! It's going to be amazing, Fred, you wait and see. Absolutely perfect!"

At Katie's commotion, Watson let out a yelp from upstairs and rushed down to inspect. I shook my head at him. "You've already claimed upstairs as your own. You're gonna be so happy for it to be turned into a bakery. So much for your diet, I won't be the only one gaining a hundred pounds."

Katie's eyes twinkled, and she bent down to rub Watson's haunch. "I haven't told anyone this, but I know the recipe for Lois's all-natural dog treats. I was going to wait and make you a bunch for Christmas. But now I'll make you a new batch every week."

At the word treat, Watson began to whine in frantic anticipation.

I grinned at the two of them. Despite not wanting a business partner, a part of me relaxed. Yes, this was right. And I'd lived enough to know that nothing was ever perfect, but that didn't mean it couldn't be wonderful.

"Well, since you brought up that word, we have to follow through. I'll go get one out of my purse." I headed toward the main counter, then paused, looking back at Katie with another thought. "You didn't really find those studies about bookstores and bakeries online, did you?"

Katie shrugged, all unconvincing innocence. "Well, if you give me five minutes, I can show them to you. You can put about anything you want to on Wikipedia."

ELEVEN

"That is just the best news, sweetie." Mom snuggled her birdlike frame against me. There were five of us crowded into a four-person booth, but thanks to her small stature, it was doable. "Oh, that reminds me." She reached below the table, snagged her purse, and began to dig through it. "I made this necklace for Katie. I'd like for you to give it to her." As she spoke, she made a pile of junk on the table. Travel-size bag of tissues, lipstick, seashells, a spool of wire, and a wide assortment of coins and pieces of lint. Finally, she pulled out a long string of clear crystals and beads, with a large smooth stone as the centerpiece. It was a muddy-dark color with a rainbow sheen over it like an oil slick. "This is labradorite. It protects against evil wishes and psychic attacks. I figured she could use it right now. I realize they're no longer thinking she's a valid suspect, but you and I both know that can change on a dime."

Barry leaned over from his spot on the other side of Mom and pulled a matching necklace outside of his tie-dyed shirt. "She made me one too. Except my stone is fluorite. It protects against sorcery and curses."

Mom gave me a knowing glance. "I was going to use black tourmaline, which is best for all-around general protection, but Barry had other ideas."

"Did you get a witch's knickers all twisted up, Barry?" Percival beamed from the other side of the table as he forked some of the fajita chicken from the sizzling plate he and Gary were sharing. "What have I told you about leaving Myrtle Bantam to herself?"

"Oh, stop." Gary elbowed him in the side. "Quit making fun of Myrtle. She's a harmless little thing."

"Harmless!" Percival screeched. "Harmless? Please don't tell me you forgot about when that sparrow flew into our store and Myrtle saw me try to encourage it back outside."

Gary cocked an eyebrow in my direction. "He was encouraging it with a broom."

"Exactly. A broom is full of twigs and sticks. Birds sit on twigs and sticks. They make nests out of them. They raise their babies in them, for crying out loud." Percival placed the fork on his plate, the chicken forgotten so he could use both of his hands.

"She was walking by and then came rushing in with both arms waving in the air, screeching and squawking and clucking like you've never heard before. It was like I was trying to kill the poor thing."

Despite himself, Gary chuckled.

So did Mom, though she swatted her brother. "Stop it. You're being unkind. And Myrtle is most definitely not a witch. She's just a lover of all things with wings and feathers. Even if she does squawk sometimes."

Having been subjected to a Myrtle Bantam squawking tirade myself, I didn't feel overly inclined to come to her reputation's rescue.

The only one who hadn't chuckled was Barry, who now shook the pendant of cloudy blues, whites, and purples at Percival. "You mock all you want, but there are forces out there that none of us are prepared to deal with. Don't come crying to me when you get cursed."

Percival did a waving motion with his finger encompassing the entirety of Barry. "Honey, you're the one dressed in head-to-toe tie-dye. Which, I hate to tell you, those pants and that shirt clash, which is saying something, considering its tie-dye. If either one of us is cursed, it's you."

Still chuckling, Mom spread her hands out over

the table, between Barry and Percival. "Now you two, save some of the drama for Christmas Day. I'm sure the grandkids wouldn't want to miss it."

"It really will be nice to have the whole family together." Gary smiled gently at Mom. "Are you sure the only thing you want us to bring is the sweet potato casserole?"

"Absolutely. Everything else is covered. Verona and Zelda are making the rest of the side dishes. Barry is in charge of appetizers, and I've got the turkey and the vegetarian roast handled." She patted my arm. "And Fred is bringing Katie, so technically, she's bringing dessert."

I wasn't the worst cook in the world, but I wasn't the kind of cook you leave in charge of something for a family gathering. "I offered to bring grilled-cheeses."

She patted my arm again. "I know you did, dear. Bringing Katie will suffice."

"What exactly is in vegetarian roast?" Percival leveled a stare at Barry once more. "Or is that the curse you're trying to guard against?"

As Percival and Barry launched back into exchanging harmless barbs, Mom put Katie's neck-lace in my hands. "I really do think it's wonderful she's opening a bakery. I bet it's just what the Cozy

Corgi needs. I'm so glad you found each other. I do wish she could have joined you for dinner tonight."

"I invited her to come, of course. But she's so over the moon that she wanted to go home and start shopping online for exactly what cooking and baking equipment she'll want to install upstairs."

Confusion crossed Mom's face. "But there's already a kitchen. I thought she could just move right in."

"So did I. But apparently not. While it worked well enough for Opal to make her edibles, it is not going to cut it for what Katie has in mind. It seems she's thinking full-on industrial-bakery-sized—" I had no idea. "—everything, it seems."

"Goodness, sounds expensive." She looked concerned and then shrugged the emotion away. "But I'm sure it will pay off. It's going to be absolute perfection."

"I hope so. She's been saving for a long time. Didn't have enough to open her own place entirely, but she has enough to redo what she needs. I'm glad we went ahead and redid the floors and walls up there. That was thanks to you."

Mom smiled and shrugged away the compliment just as easily as she had the concern. "So glad you're here, darling. I hope this new life treats you better than the old one."

I bent down awkwardly to give her a quick kiss on the cheek. "It already is, Mom. It already is." The truth of those words hit me, surrounded by the older generation of my family, as we were all squished into a brightly painted booth at Habanero's, Barry and Percival still bickering, and Gary simply enjoying the show. Even with the drama since I moved into town, I was certain this was the life I not only needed, but wanted.

We continued eating for a while, the conversation ranging from speculation about the first lawsuit Noah and Jonah would have over their Christmas garland, to listing the gifts they were getting for the grandkids so no one got the same thing, to their hopes of what would happen to the empty shops next to the Cozy Corgi.

By the time the sopaipillas were delivered, I didn't think I could eat a bite more. But sure enough, I managed, and before long my fingers were sticky with honey.

Mom had just stuffed another bite into her mouth when she looked over and stiffened slightly. I followed her gaze.

Gerald Jackson, who was nearly as wide as he

was tall, was making his way from across the restaurant toward our booth. She leaned in to me, uncharacteristically speaking with her mouth full. "Be nice, Fred."

I was a woman pushing forty and yet could still get reprimanded by my mother for not even doing anything. It was like she knew me.

"Howdy there, boys! So good to see you!" Gerald nearly trumpeted over the background music as he reached us.

All three of the men in our booth let out similar sounds of greeting, and there were rounds of handshakes and backslapping.

When the male camaraderie died down a bit, he tipped his hat in Mom's and my direction. "Always a pleasure to see you, ladies."

I managed a noncommittal nod, and my mother a sweet "You too, of course, Gerald. Happy holidays."

Maybe someday I'd be as gracious as my mother. But I doubted it.

"And to you, Phyllis. I'm sure you're glad to have your girl back."

"That's very true, Gerald. It's nice to have the family together at Christmastime again." And though her other hand reached out and slid over Barry's leg under the table, I was certain that a part of her was also thinking of my father. I often felt he was still watching over us, also pleased that we were all together.

Pleasantries exchanged, Gerald refocused on the men at the table. He started to squat slightly to rest his elbow on the table to be closer, then, finding that difficult, seemed to think better of it and stood straight once more. "Terrible business with the Diamonds. Just terrible." He patted his chest. "Just breaks your heart, all that Duncan has sacrificed and this is where it leads."

It took all my willpower to keep from pointing out that Gerald was the reason Declan had managed to get his father declared incompetent. Having Mom pressed against me probably didn't hurt.

There was a round of agreement from the table. "And then that scene the night before last at the Chinese restaurant." Percival *tsked*. "And to such a charming, beautiful girl like Daphne. After all Declan's years of philandering, she deserved better."

Somehow in the chaos of it all, I'd never passed on to them about Dolan and Daphne. Well, I definitely wasn't going to do so with Gerald Jackson in our midst.

Gerald nodded his agreement with Percival. "That is true, but I take it you haven't heard the latest?" His wild eyebrows rose nearly halfway up his bald head as he leered over his glasses at each man in turn.

All three of them shook their heads. Mom and I didn't bother.

This time, Gerald managed to support his weight with his hands on the edge of the table as he leaned nearer. "Well, with Declan's death, certain things came to light. One of which was he changed his will, less than a week ago, in fact."

Barry, Percival, and Gary all sat silently with their mouths open, waiting. It was Mom who ushered him forward. "Well, do you know how he changed it?"

He looked at her in surprise, like he'd forgotten Mom was there. Then cleared his throat as if uncertain he should continue with the gossip.

It was a good thing the waitress had taken Gary and Percival's sizzling cast-iron fajita plate away. I would have been tempted to smash it over his head.

"Don't worry about Mom and I being delicate, Gerald. We handled things the night Barry was arrested for Opal's murder. All on our own, if you remember." To my surprise, Mom didn't elbow me or anything. Gerald, who acted as Barry's lawyer—and apparently every other man over the age of fifty in

Estes Park—had been so late that all the drama had been over, all because he had to drive to his little house in Glen Haven for a bottle of his homemade kombucha.

"Ah, yes. Well...." Gerald blinked rapidly a few times and then once more promptly forgot Mom and I were there. His gaze darted back and forth between Gary and Percival but then finally came to rest on Barry, seemingly judging him to be the most worthy of the news. "As I've been told, the original will left the entire business to Daphne and Dolan. Those two, of course, would take care of Duncan, just as always." He pulled his glasses farther down his nose and leaned in even closer to Barry. "But now, he's left everything, and I do mean everything, to Sarah Margaret Beeman."

"You're kidding! He left it all to another woman?" Percival gasped, startling Gerald. "Now *that's* a scandal!" Gary nodded his agreement.

"Poor Duncan. Poor, poor Duncan." Barry just sounded sad. "And Daphne and Dolan too. He managed to betray his entire family."

Gerald nodded his agreement. "I don't see how such a thing would hold up in court, but it is Declan."

I couldn't imagine it holding up in court either,

although, with Gerald defending the rest of the Diamonds, who knew...

After a few moments in silence, Mom spoke up, her voice timid. "Who's Sarah Beeman? I don't think I've ever heard of her."

"No idea." Gerald shrugged. "That's part of what makes it so confusing. No one knows her."

I did. I almost said so, then stopped myself.

Maybe I didn't. Sarah Beeman. It sounded so familiar. I knew that name. If it hadn't been for the reaction of the others around the table, I would've assumed it was someone I'd met downtown as I was trying to clear Barry or Katie. But if that were the case, all of them would've known who she was. There was no one in town I knew that they didn't. So I must not know her.

But I did know that name. I was sure of it.

And talk about opening it wide for motive. If any of the Diamonds had known about the will, it would definitely be a reason to murder Declan. It seemed their reasons were almost limitless.

TWELVE

I expected to see Katie the following morning when Watson and I stopped in for our daily chai and scone at the Black Bear Roaster. Instead, Carla, looking impossibly more pregnant than the day before, met us with a glare from behind the counter. "Pumpkin spice latte and gingerbread scone like normal, correct?"

She'd waited on me once, hardly enough time to have established a normal order. "You know, I think I'm going to mix it up, be crazy today." I gave her a wink, and the second I did, I felt weird about it. Perhaps I thought it would cheer her up; though why a wink would do it, I had no idea. "How about let's try a large dirty chai and a pumpkin scone."

Carla shrugged. "You got it."

As she made the drink, I glanced behind the counter and only found a thin teenage boy refilling the coffee grinder, probably working during his

Christmas vacation. In less than two minutes, Carla was back, sliding me my chai along with a piece of pumpkin bread. I nearly corrected her mistake, then thought maybe she was doing me a favor. I was the one insane enough to keep ordering scones and expecting them to change. "Thanks so much. Ah, I thought Katie would be here."

Carla halted, the credit card I'd given her frozen in midair. "She called me late last night, gave her two weeks' notice. Apparently she's opening her own bakery." She sniffed. "I told her to not bother coming in. She was a weird one, anyway. Although I regretted that decision at five this morning, let me tell you." Carla rubbed her belly.

I paused for a second, waiting for tirade against me and my bookshop, but none came. It seemed Katie hadn't mentioned where she was opening her bakery, and I was grateful.

A minute or so later, and Watson and I were headed across the street to the Cozy Corgi. I took a bite of the pumpkin bread, which was mildly moister than the scones, and tossed Watson a bite when we reached the other sidewalk. We were almost to the store when I realized my dilemma over whether to continue going to the Black Bear Roaster would be short-lived. Soon dirty chais and non-dry scones would be right above my head every morning. The thought felt like a mental cozy blanket pulled up over me. Life was going to be wonderful. Endless caffeine, endless pastries, and endless books.

Dear Lord, I'd be lucky if it was only a hundred pounds I gained.

To my surprise, even after the pumpkin bread was gone, Watson didn't trundle up the steps and disappear to the second floor as normal. Instead he wandered over to the nonfiction section that Katie and I had arranged the day before, and fell asleep in the rays of the winter sunlight pouring through the window. As rare as that was, I knew I should enjoy it while it lasted. As soon as Katie was baking upstairs, I'd never see Watson again.

As I worked on arranging the biography section, careful not to wake Watson, I pondered the implications of Declan leaving everything to the mystery woman. I was of two minds on the situation. It made sense for any of the three remaining Diamonds to be so angry at Declan that they would murder him. But Declan had made other enemies, hadn't he? Even if not as obvious as his family drama, there were other possibilities.

And who in the world was the mystery woman? Everyone knew everything about everyone in a town as small as Estes Park, or at least thought they did. The only possibility I could imagine was that the woman must not be from here. Maybe from Denver or Lyons?

I was nearly done with the third box of books when I realized what day it was. I looked over at a peacefully sleeping Watson as guilt and dread washed over me. Today was the day I'd agreed to the corgi playdate with Paulie Mertz. I was tempted to find an excuse. I was opening a store, for crying out loud. If I could use it for an excuse to refrain from a dinner with a handsome park ranger, I should definitely be able to do it to keep Watson away from Flotsam and Jetsam. But I really just wanted to get it over with.

Katie called around lunchtime, sounding ecstatic about the abrupt dismissal from the coffee shop. She'd gone down to Denver to check out industrial baking equipment in person, as opposed to online, and needed me to get some measurements from the upstairs kitchen.

Then, after a lunch of leftover Mexican food from the night before for myself, and a can of tuna for Watson—how he could tell the difference between canned dog food and canned tuna, I would never know—it was back to work and pondering over who the mystery woman was. It wasn't long before I had a new suspect. Sarah Beeman, whoever she was, certainly had a motive—she was in line to inherit everything.

As the afternoon wore on, pondering Declan's killing gave way to a buildup of dread of the corgi playdate. With less than an hour to spare, I grew more and more tempted to cancel. And with every moment that passed, it would make it ever more rude. I was so caught up in my thoughts that I let out a yelp when the mail was shoved through the slot in the door.

Watson beat me to it, sniffing the pile of mail like he expected either a snack or a bomb, then gave me a withering glare when I walked over and picked it up. It was all junk. How it was possible that a new business, one that hadn't even opened, could get so many catalogs and applications for credit cards was beyond me. I was nearly ready to toss it all into the recycling when I noticed the letter stuck in the pages of a floral catalog.

My skin tingled as I read the envelope: *Sarah M. Beeman.*

The rest of the mail fell from my fingers with a clatter on the floor, and a yelp from Watson. I barely noticed.

Sarah M. Beeman. *That* was why I had recognized the name.

What was the name Gerald had said? Sarah Margaret Beeman.

And as before, the return address was a Denver law firm.

It still didn't make sense, but at least I knew I wasn't going crazy.

I checked my cell, half an hour before I was to meet Paulie. Another second passed and I made up my mind. I grabbed the leash off the counter and patted my thigh. "Come on, Watson. We've gotta make this quick."

When we reached Rocky Mountain Imprints, we were thwarted. Two burly men were blocking the entrance as they did something to the doorframe. Only then did I notice the glass that made up the center of the door was missing. Repairmen, obviously. I nearly decided to wait, to come back later, but the prospect of being with Paulie and his two crazed corgis while this was on my mind sounded like the epitome of torture. I motioned toward the empty space.

"Sorry to bother you. Do you mind if we pop in

for a moment? I hate to get in your way, but I promise I'll be quick."

Though both looked annoyed, one of the men opened what remained of the door and allowed Watson and I to walk in.

"Thank you so much!"

We barely rounded the corner into the store, when Peg saw us. "Oh, hi! So nice of you to drop by. I was planning on heading down to you in a few minutes."

That threw me off. "You were coming to see me?"

She tilted her cute blonde head. "Well, of course, silly. You're the client. Or potential one, at least." She winked, then raised her voice and hollered toward the back. "Joe, sweetie, bring up Fred's hoodie, would you?"

The hoodie! I'd completely forgotten. Peg had said it would be done by today.

She turned her attention back to me. "It came out super cute. I really hope you'll be pleased. I chose a soft brown background. I think it goes nicely with the white lettering."

A man just as large as the two repairmen out front, walked into view from the back of the store and handed Peg the folded hoodie. "Here you go, love." His voice was deep and soft. The picture of them together was somewhat off-putting. Peg so small, and Joe absolutely huge. And where Peg was beautiful in a pixie sort of way, the same could not be said for Joe, in any sort of way. The man was unfortunately homely. He gave me a polite nod, then disappeared back through the racks of T-shirts.

Peg unfolded the hoodie and grinned as she inspected it, then turned it toward me. The size I'd ordered for myself looked nearly like a tent next to her petite stature. And for a moment, all my other concerns vanished, and I sighed. She'd been right. The logo was perfect on the soft brown background of the hoodie. Like on the sign of my store, a fat corgi sat on the top of the stack of four books, with the words *The Cozy Corgi* arched over its head. I reached out and touched the corgi with my fingertip. It was still warm. Joe must've just finished making it. I couldn't seem to tear my gaze away. "Oh, Peg, it's wonderful."

"I'm glad you think so. I really do think they'll be a big seller for you. Especially if you do a variety of products. I know you weren't in love with the idea of shot glasses, but there's other things to choose from." She folded up the hoodie, slipped it into a bag, and handed it to me. "This one's on the house. Wear it a couple days, give it some washes, see the quality of it, and let me know. We'd love to be your supplier."

I was glad she mentioned washing it first. I'd been ready to sign on the dotted line. Bakery upstairs or not, I'd find a place somewhere for Cozy Corgi merchandise. Even if I was the only customer. "Thank you, Peg. I'm sure it will be just fine, but I'll try it out and let you know."

Just then there was a loud crash, causing Peg, Watson, and myself to jump.

A deep voice rumbled embarrassingly from the front door. "Sorry! My bad. We'll cut a new piece of glass. It'll just take a little bit longer."

"No problem." Peg called to them and then looked at me with a commiserating sigh. "Business ownership isn't all glitz and glam, as you're about to find out. Some kid must've hit our front door with a BB gun yesterday, and it's turned into this big old thing. Expensive, but not enough to turn in to the insurance without our premiums going up. Always something." She shook her head.

"I know what you mean. When I came up here, I thought I'd spend a week or so and have my shop open. By the time we finally do, it will be almost two months. And that's still a big if I can get it ready by January."

She shrugged. "It's not a big deal if you don't. You'll be missing some money during the winter months, but not a ton. Just make sure you're up and running by the end of May. Our biggest season is when kids are out of school. Then it's every man for himself. We each have to make enough over the summer to last us the entire year."

Thanks to the betrayal of my best friend and the dollar amount of compensation I received, even though it wasn't what it should have been, I didn't have to worry about sales to the same level as many of the other storeowners. Otherwise, I never in a million years would have opened a brick-and-mortar bookshop. I figured it best not to mention that, though.

"Thanks for the advice. Any insight I can get into operating a store in a tourist town is priceless." I repositioned the bag with the hoodie in preparation to leave and then remembered why I'd come in the first place. I held the envelope out to her. "Oh, silly me. I almost forgot. I got another misdelivered piece of mail."

She took it, read the envelope, and her eyes widened slightly. She glanced toward the back again. Before a heartbeat passed, she smiled up at me. "Mis-delivered mail will be the least of your headaches as a business owner, I can promise you." She tucked the letter away. "Thanks for bringing this. And while I don't expect you to handle our mail, if you see any more letters addressed to her, feel free to throw them away."

Odd request. "Who is she? I've met a lot of people in town but haven't met anyone named Sarah Beeman."

Peg rolled her eyes. "That's what I mean. Even small things add up to large annoyances. I don't know who she is. We've gotten letters addressed to her since the time we opened the store. I can only assume she was someone who owned the shop in this location before, or maybe someone who worked here. I don't know." She cleared her throat and glanced toward the back once more. "I tried to find her the first couple of times, and then gave up. I suppose I need to contact the post office and let them know that if they come across any more letters to her to just return them to the sender."

"Well, I know she has to be around here." I wasn't going to share all that I knew, but maybe a tidbit of gossip could loosen the wheels, or trigger a memory that she might tell me later. "The Diamonds next door know her."

She flinched, then shook her head. "They do? I

don't think that's true. I asked everyone around when I got that first letter to her. Including the Diamonds. They didn't know."

"That's strange. I'm certain Declan knew her."

Peg just shook her head. "Maybe so. The Diamonds are a wonderful family, but Declan and I never got along." A flush rose to her cheeks. "I'm sorry. I forgot. One shouldn't speak such things of the dead. God rest his soul."

That most definitely wasn't a tenet I lived by, but I nodded along anyway. "No problem." I held the bag with the hoodie up. "Thank you again for this. I absolutely love it. I'm certain I'll want some other things in my store."

She smiled, but not as brightly as before. "I'm so glad. It will be a lot of fun working with you. Do let me know what you've decided, and of course if you have any questions, never hesitate."

With a wave, I turned to leave, but as we approached the door, there was still glass everywhere. One of the repairman looked at me and simply shook his head. I glanced over to Peg. "Do you have a back exit? I suppose I could pick Watson up and carry him over the glass, but he hates it. And I'm covered in enough dog hair as it is. Anytime I pick him up, I might as well be wearing a corgi fur coat after."

"Oh, my goodness. I wasn't even thinking. I'm so sorry." She rushed around the counter and waved me toward her, then pointed to a door in the back that was barely visible through all the T-shirts hanging in the way. "Right through there, sweetie. That's the alley. It leads to the new riverwalk out back." She reached up to pat my shoulder, and then bent to offer a similar gesture to Watson, who scooted quickly out of her reach.

"Thank you. Never mind Watson; he's always a little grumpy. Unless you're my stepfather, and then you're Christmas morning and birthdays all rolled into one." My stepfather *and* Leo Lopez, it seemed.

She waved me off. "Not a big deal. I have a cat at home that is the exact same way. Absolutely worships the ground Joe walks on. I might as well be kitty litter for all she is concerned."

And with a final wave, Watson and I wove our way through the maze of T-shirts, past another trophy case with a baseball bat leaning beside it, and out the back door. Though the day was cloudy, it was bright, and I had to blink, letting my eyes adjust. Once I did, the alley looked strangely familiar, and glancing behind, the answer of why was obvious. It was the alley that Rocky Mountain Imprints shared with Bushy Evergreen's Workshop. The alley where I'd seen Daphne and Dolan kiss two days before.

The toyshop had still been closed as Watson and I had passed it to get to Peg's, and I was tempted to go knock on their back door. Though what I would ask if somebody answered, I had no idea. If one of them did know who Sarah Beeman was and they were Declan's killer, asking them in an alley wouldn't be the smartest move. And with a jolt, I suddenly remembered Paulie Mertz and his eel-like corgis. I glanced at my cell. We were almost late.

I barely noticed Watson tugging on my leash, until he let out a sharp yelp and a whine.

I hurried over and found him chewing on something on the side of the dumpster. "Watson. Stop it."

He yelped again, but kept right on chewing on his treasure. Probably a sharp bone.

I squatted down beside him, and pulled whatever it was from his mouth. "You are ridiculous. Only you would continue to eat something that's hurting you. Actual dog food, you're too good to eat, but this" — I shook it at him, sparing it a glance —"old work glove is a delicacy all of the sudden." I narrowed my eyes at the glove. There was something red and chunky all over it.

Unperturbed, Watson darted back at the pile of refuse that had fallen from the dumpster and began chomping down on something else.

"Oh, for crying out loud." I yanked his leash away, far enough to see that he'd discovered a fourth of a pizza. Of course, he'd been attempting to eat a glove because it was covered in pizza sauce. Brilliant. I gave another tug, but Watson was strong enough that when he made up his mind, moving him wasn't a one-handed job. I tossed the glove back by the pizza, and pulled him away, both hands tight around his leash. We were out of the alley before he stopped struggling.

He glared up at me, making it very clear that there would be no corgi cuddles later.

"Give me that look all you want to, buddy. All you did was just make me feel not the least bit bad for you about what's to happen next. I was planning on making you play with Flotsam and Jetsam for thirty minutes at the most. But I think you deserve to have to play with them for an hour."

Even as we made our way to the park, I knew that was one threat I wouldn't follow through on. No way in the world was I spending the entire hour in solitary conversation with Paulie Mertz.

THIRTEEN

Watson whined the entire two-block walk from the alley to the park. "Complain all you want to. I'm not going to have any sympathy, Mr. Stubborn Pants." The pathetic look he gave me already had me softening, like he knew it would. "Maybe just fifteen minutes with the evil twins, how about that?" Though how in the world I was going to get away with only fifteen minutes without seeming like the rudest person in the entire universe, I wasn't sure.

With one block to spare, the winter night sky opened up and snow began to come down in torrents. I lifted my gaze skyward. "Thank you for the Christmas miracle, Santa." I could blame the Mini Cooper, say that it didn't have four-wheel drive. That much was true, so it wouldn't be a lie. Hopefully Paulie wouldn't know that Mini Coopers came with front wheel drive, and it was doing just splendidly in the mountains so far.

I did a double take when I noticed Paulie and Flotsam and Jetsam at the playground across the street. When he'd suggested meeting at a park, I'd pictured a dog park, or at least a large area with trees, open space, and paths. This was a kids' playground, and a tiny one at that. Though I supposed it was my own fault; he'd clearly said meet at the park close to the intersection of Elkhorn Avenue and East Riverside Drive, down by the river. It was in the middle of shops. I supposed I just hadn't been thinking. Well, one more plausible excuse. Watson needed to run, get out his energy.

I nearly snorted out a laugh at the thought. Watson and I had the same outlook on running. Something dangerous needed to be chasing us, or there had to be a really good meal at the finish line. Other than that, he'd sooner help unbox books than run.

Paulie waved frantically as we crossed the street, like we couldn't see him. Both Flotsam and Jetsam followed suit and bounded at the end of their leashes.

Watson whimpered.

"I know, buddy. I know. Maybe ten minutes."

As we drew nearer, both the corgis crashed into Watson and me, and Paulie pulled me into a hug. In truth, the hug wasn't very effective as he still had a hand on each of the hyperactive dogs' leashes, but I was grateful, as it made it shorter, even if a touch more awkward. "Fred, it's so nice of you to join us for a playdate. I didn't expect you to show up. I've tried doggy playdates with a couple of other dog owners in town, and... well...."

He looked such a combination of embarrassed and happy that I readjusted mentally. Fifteen minutes. A person could stand anything for fifteen minutes, right?

For the life of me, I couldn't think of a thing to say. Watson bashed into the back of my legs, saving me from having to figure it out. Looking down, Flotsam and Jetsam were still bounding up and down, this time frequently landing on Watson's paws. Disentangling myself, I pulled Watson along with me and took a seat on one of the swings.

It took Paulie a few seconds to follow as he untangled his corgis' leashes, offering Watson a brief respite.

"For some reason, I was picturing a dog park or something. I don't know why, I've driven past this a million times, but there's not much space for them, is there?"

Paulie gave a little shrug, and even in the

shadowy lights from the cloudy evening, I could make out embarrassment over his face. "Well. I thought you wouldn't show. Like I said, that's happened before. There is a dog park, but it's a farther walk. So I thought we'd meet here, just in case you canceled, not so far to go." His smile brightened. "But the next time, we can meet there." The cheerfulness lasted a total of three seconds, and then his features crashed once more. "No, we can't. Flotsam and Jetsam have been banned from that dog park." He perked up again. I didn't think I'd ever seen such speedy mood shifts. "But you could come to my house. Plenty of room for the dogs to play."

Oh dear Lord, so much for Christmas miracles. One of the other dogs bumped into Watson, he yelped and then growled, which was much sooner than he normally did with other corgis. But a perfect excuse. "Sorry, Paulie. As you can see, Watson really doesn't get into playing all that much. He kinda just eats and sleeps and casts judgmental glances at other dogs and people walking by. That's kind of his thing."

Paulie only looked daunted for a second. "Well, you could come over for dinner." He must've seen the answer rising to my lips, and he rushed ahead.

"You could bring Watson, of course. I could put Flotsam and Jetsam in my bedroom. It wouldn't be a problem."

Dinner? And this was why I should've turned this down from the beginning, even if I would've felt guilty. I reached out to take his hand, then realized what I was doing and folded my hand in my lap over Watson's leash. "Paulie. That's very sweet, and you're very.... That's very sweet. But I want to be clear up front. I'm not looking for dates or a relationship. I have my hands full starting a business. I'm sorry."

"No, no, no!" Paulie waved both his hands, causing Flotsam and Jetsam's leashes to tremble, and setting them both off on a barking tirade. "I didn't mean as a date. Goodness, I know you're out of my league. Plus I hear you and Sergeant Wexler are an item. Course then I noticed you and that park ranger fellow outside of Carl and Anna's the other day, so maybe not."

He'd just thrown so much information at me at once, that again I was speechless. He'd noticed me and Leo? And even Paulie Mertz had heard the rumors about Branson and me? This time I did reach out and put my hand over his, despite my better instincts. "Paulie, it has nothing to do with leagues or anything like that." I pulled my hand back.

He snorted, but it wasn't a sarcastic sound. "Oh, please, Fred. You're so far out of my league, it's ridiculous. But I truly wasn't asking for a date. I know I'm not really supposed to make friendships, but I'm just... lonely. I promise, that's all."

I believed him. He truly did look lonely and sad. And seemed like he was hurting. Some of his words came back to me and struck me as odd. "What do you mean you're not supposed to make friends? What kind of rule is that?"

His eyes widened. "Oh, I didn't even mean to say that. Nothing. I just meant..." I could swear he was searching for something to say, some excuse. "Well, I don't exactly fit in most places. My teeth are stained. I often smell like fish water from cleaning the aquariums. I get nervous and start to sweat, even in a snowstorm, and I frequently get nosebleeds."

There was growling and snapping at our feet, and I leaned forward ready to pull Watson to safety, but it was simply Flotsam and Jetsam playing together, apparently having finally given up on Watson developing a playful personality.

That was a relief.

I turned back to Paulie and placed my hand over his again. "Oh, Paulie. I couldn't tell you were sweating, and I've never noticed you get a nosebleed." As soon as the words left my lips, I realized that I'd addressed the wrong part of his statement. I should've argued against the yellow teeth and the smell of fish tank, but it was too late to try to cover that up. Plus, the man had a mirror. I couldn't exactly tell him his teeth weren't stained.

Even so, he smiled like I'd just paid him the highest compliment.

Despite the truth of his list of social faux pas, it still didn't explain the friendship comment he'd made before. There was something there. But I didn't push.

I checked on Watson again. He seemed to be contentedly licking his paws as he continued to be forgotten by the other two corgis. I refocused on Paulie. "I'm sorry you're having a difficult time. I know it's hard being new in town."

He gave me a knowing look. "You're much newer to town than I am, and you're not making it look difficult."

Just as I was searching for something else to say, Watson let out another yelp, this one sounding like pain, and once more I was ready to pull him back from the others. But they weren't bothering him. He gave his paw a lick, and then yelped again. I reached down, took the paw he'd been licking, and ran my fingers gently around it, feeling the pads. There was nothing, and Watson didn't flinch as I touched his paw, like he would've if there was a thorn or splinter. His tongue darted out to lick his nose, and he let out another pain-filled yip, sneezed, and then yipped again. He was clearly hurting.

My heart rate shooting up, I whipped off the swing and knelt in front of him. "What is it, sweetie? What's wrong?"

He let out another whimper of pain.

I gently tried to lift his head to see into his mouth, but it was too dark. As I fished in my purse, trying to find my cell, Flotsam and Jetsam crashed into my back like I was playing.

"Boys! Stop!" Paulie stood and pulled them away quickly, then tied them to a leg of the jungle gym, just out of reach, and then he was back. "Sorry about that."

"It's fine." I found my cell, switched on the flashlight feature, and handed it to Paulie. "Would you hold this for me? Angle toward Watson's mouth."

He did, and in the light, I could see just how

wild Watson's eyes were. I'd never seen him look like that.

I reached for his muzzle, attempted to raise the lip enough to see his teeth, to see if he had something cutting into him. He yelped in pain again and pulled his head away with a warning growl. I pulled my hand away, and my breath caught as I noticed blood over my fingertips. I looked up at Paulie. "Something's wrong. I gotta get him to the vet. I have to go."

"Of course. Of course." Paulie handed me my cell. "They're closed by this time of night, but they have an emergency number, and I know the vet. Want me to call them and let them know you're on your way?"

Gratitude rushed over me. "Yes, that would be wonderful. Thank you." And then all my attention was on Watson. I took his leash and gave him a gentle pull. He stood tentatively and took a few steps, seemed pain-free, and then sneezed again. He howled in agony, then trailed off to a whimper.

I bent down, scooped all thirty-three pounds of him into my arms, and ran as smoothly as I could to my car.

. . .

The veterinarian, Dr. Sallee pulled into the parking lot moments behind me. Though we hadn't met before, he didn't bother with paperwork or formality, which I appreciated. He got the clinic up and running as he asked the expected information-seeking questions. Had Watson had an injury? Had there been some sort of impact? Had he been eating normally? Frequent and regular bowel movements? Was he up to date on shots?

It wasn't until we had Watson on his examining table that he asked the magic question. "Has he gotten into any trash recently?"

"No, of course not." I yanked my hair away that had fallen into my eyes, and felt close to tears. Then it came back to me. "Wait, yes. Probably... less than an hour ago, maybe half an hour ago. We were in the alley behind the T-shirt shop. Watson found leftover pizza."

"Pizza shouldn't do that unless it was rancid. But then he'd be sick, not in pain." Dr. Sallee refocused on Watson. "You're sure his pain is from his mouth?"

"Yes. That's the only place. Nothing's wrong with his feet. He doesn't let on when I touch his belly or anything."

The vet refocused on Watson and reached out to touch his muzzle. Watson growled and tried to get away. "I'll need you to hold him. If I can look in his mouth without him biting me, I will. Otherwise I'll need to figure out a different way. I'd rather not give him sedation since we don't know what's happening."

Feeling like a traitor, I bent over the examining table and fixed Watson in place with my arms and body weight. "I'm so sorry, baby. I'm so sorry."

Watson struggled a little, but actually seemed more at ease with my presence around him. He snarled as Dr. Sallee reached for his muzzle again, but didn't move to bite. Though there was a low grumbling growl radiating through him the entire time, he allowed the vet to lift his lips and inspect his gum.

The vet's voice was low enough I could barely hear it. "He's bleeding, but I don't see anything causing it. Nothing looks infected. But...." He cocked his head and leaned a little closer, then angled his light a different way. "What in the world...?" He retrieved a long tweezer and then was back, once more twisting his head, getting the lighting just right, as if he couldn't quite see whatever it was, and then he darted the tweezers inside and pulled something nearly microscopic and bloody out of Watson's mouth. He held it up between us, his eyes narrowed. "This was stuck in his gums. I'm not sure what it is."

I wasn't either.

After walking over to the sink, he filled a glass with water and then dipped the tweezers inside. He stirred it around, then pulled the object back out and returned it to the light between us. "I still have no idea."

"Neither do—" Dr. Sallee twisted the object slightly, and in so doing, the bright green of the shirt under his lab coat somehow reflected in it and I realized what it was. A shard from Noah and Jonah's garland. "It's fiberglass. It's from Christmas garland."

He looked puzzled but only for a second, and then his eyes grew wide. "Oh, that flashy kind that a couple of the stores have up this year?"

I nodded. "Exactly."

He grimaced. "Nasty stuff." He stroked Watson's head. "Who knows how long that's been floating around in there just waiting for the chance to get stuck. Better check and see if there's some more."

There were. Five other pieces. Three of them embedded, two caught in the folds of the skin of his inner cheek. The doctor also gave me a prescription that would help sweep away any fragments that might have entered Watson's digestive tract.

"Make sure he takes it easy tomorrow. And if you notice any changes at all, give me a call. I don't predict anything happening, not with that medicine, but if there should be any bleeding or he's not eating normally any time over the next three or four days, I want to know immediately. Even if it's Christmas. Strange that he'd get into that."

FOURTEEN

Watson was asleep on the passenger seat when I pulled in front of the house. After sliding the car into Park, I stared at the twenty feet between us and the front porch. When I first moved to Estes, I was still such a city girl that I let Watson have free rein in the yard, just like I had in Kansas City. Then Leo mentioned how common it was for pets to be snagged by mountain lions and other wildlife, sometimes when right beside their human. Since then, we used a leash from car to cabin. We'd removed his collar at the veterinary office, and the thought of putting it back on with those stupid scratchy pieces of garland possibly in his throat was more than I could bear. But I also wasn't willing to risk him walking by my side, this time of night especially.

I got out of the car, walked around to the passenger side, and cracked open the door so Watson wouldn't jump out if he woke up suddenly. Sure enough, his tired eyes opened and blinked at me. Wedging myself in, I opened the door a little farther, and wrapped my arms around him.

Watson let out an annoyed huff as I lifted him, offered a halfhearted squirm, and then stilled, allowing me to carry him. "Oh, baby. You really don't feel good, do you?" I was going to murder my brothers-in-law.

Once inside, I closed the door with my foot and gently carried him over and placed him by the armchair, intending to light a fire and sit with him.

Watson blinked again, looked around, and then stood. He gave a small stretch, and then padded off toward the bedroom. I followed. He curled up in his dog bed which was directly beside my four-poster. Then he let out a contented sigh.

That made me feel better. If he had an opinion of where he wanted to sleep at that moment, he at least felt well enough to be himself. I lay on the floor, curled up beside him as best I could, and softly stroked his fur. I intended to lull him to sleep, letting him know he wasn't alone. In less than two minutes, Watson glared at me through slitted eyes, gave a little huff, stood, and repositioned to lay the other direction.

Laughing, I placed a quick kiss on the top of his head. "Yup, you're going to be fine."

Even so, I knew sleep was a long way off. If it was going to come at all. The thoughts of fiberglass shards inside of him scared me to death. Thank goodness some had caught in his mouth, otherwise I might never have known until it was too late. I got onto the bed and curled on my side so I could keep watch over him.

I couldn't lose Watson. I just couldn't. He'd quite literally walked into my life at one of my darkest moments since my father's death. Came right up to me, shoved his little corgi forehead against mine as I knelt and sobbed, my hands covering my face. Looking back, it was such a completely un-Watson-like thing to do. From that moment on, things got better. I didn't have any notion that my father had been reincarnated into the form of a corgi or any such nonsense, but I did feel like Dad had given me a gift. A reminder he was watching, that he loved me.

It had been an added bonus that Watson possessed such a strong, and at times obstinate, personality. He was the kind of dog my father would've loved. He wasn't one to try to impress. If anything, he expected the opposite. It was up to the rest of the world to impress *him*. Dad would've liked that quality, and it only made me more certain that he'd picked Watson especially for me.

I couldn't lose Watson.

As I lay there watching him, I realized I was actually a little angry with him, not unlike times I'd felt after my father had been murdered. Those ridiculous moments where I raged at him for having the audacity of getting killed, for leaving me and Mom. And now Watson, so stubborn about not eating dog food, demanding human food in all its forms, had decided to eat the world's most deadly Christmas garland, of all things. It simply didn't make any sense. None.

Maybe if I had anything in my house or the shop, and some of it had broken off and fallen into his food and he hadn't realized... it would make sense. But I didn't have any of it. Maybe at my mother's and Barry's during family dinner? As soon as that thought entered, I let it go. That had been days before. He wouldn't still have pieces floating around in his mouth. It had to be fresh, had to be today.

Maybe it was in the pizza in the alley behind the toy store. They had the garland. Maybe they'd torn it all down and thrown it away and some had gotten into the pizza.

The answer was so obvious, and it crashed into

me so hard, that I simultaneously felt stupid and stunned. Not the pizza.

The glove.

I sat up. The large workmen's glove Watson had been chewing on. The one with the red-stained pizza sauce on it.

I drummed my fingers on the duvet as I thought, each new notion crashing like another wave over me. What if it wasn't just pizza? What if it had been blood? I glanced down at Watson. He'd been chewing on the glove. If he'd gotten bits of the garland from the glove, then he just found what Declan's murderer had used to help strangle him.

By the dumpster? It seemed rather careless.

That part didn't matter. I was certain that was what it was. And right behind Bushy Evergreen's Workshop. It was the only thing needed to figure out which one of the Diamonds had killed Declan.

I called Branson. He didn't answer, so I left a voicemail. Then I texted him a few minutes later. I tried to call again.

After ten minutes, I couldn't take it anymore, and I called the station.

There was an answer after one ring. "Police, what is your emergency?"

"No emergency, but I have information on the

Declan Diamond murder. Could I speak to Sergeant Wexler?"

There was a brief pause, and the clicking of keys. "I'm sorry, Sergeant Wexler's not on duty. But I'll get you through to the officer in charge of this case." Before I could protest, she put me on hold, and silence filled my ears, an occasional beep let me know the connection was still live. I had a sinking feeling about who was going to pick up. Sure enough, nearly three score of electronic beeps later, Susan Green's voice greeted my ears. "This is Officer Green. I hear you have information on the Diamond case."

I nearly hung up the phone. I had my thumb over the End Call button and then envisioned her tracing the call and how that would look. I lifted the phone back to my ear. "Yes. I do. I think I discovered the glove the killer wore to be able to use the garland to strangle Declan."

She groaned. "Fred?"

"Yes. This is Fred."

"So you found a glove, huh?" I swore I could hear the eye roll. "Just one? Was this killer doing the moonwalk at the same time as the strangling?"

"Maybe there's two. I didn't check." I was

surprised my voice was audible through my gritted teeth.

"Really? I thought you were better at police work than the rest of us. You know, the rest of us who are actually... *police*."

"I never said that." Watson groaned in his sleep, and I realized my voice had risen. I didn't think I'd ever met anyone other than my ex-husband who could make me so angry so quickly. "May I speak to Branson... sorry, Sergeant Wexler?"

"What's wrong, Fred? Lovers' spat? He finally realize you're just as batty as the rest of your family and refused to take your calls?"

It was her soft chuckle that did it.

I saw red.

"You know what, that's exactly what happened." I ended the call.

Well, that was stupid. She'd just call back and then give me a hard time for hanging up on an officer of the law. How she'd ever earned such a title was beyond me. Although it wasn't, really. Cops like her had been the bane of my father's career.

I waited for her to call back. To my surprise, she didn't.

After a few moments of considering calling her, I pushed the thought aside. Even if she did actually listen to me, I didn't trust her to follow through on it, and if she did, she'd probably find some way to use it against Katie, my parents, or myself.

I could go get the glove. Easy enough. As I started to slide off the bed, Watson gave another moan in his sleep, this one seeming like he was having a pleasant dream.

No, I wasn't going to leave him, and I wasn't going to carry him back to the car. I wasn't going to risk anything happening to him. And chances were, the glove was fine. No one knew I'd seen it, and that alley was on the same side as my shop. Trash pickup wouldn't be for another three days.

Besides, Branson would call back. He'd listen.

Lying there, I nearly vibrated with excitement and nerves. One step closer to figuring out who killed Declan, one step closer to truly and completely clearing Katie's name. And though maybe I should be ashamed of the thought, one step closer to me figuring this thing out. The next thought, I was certain I should be ashamed of. I had a sense of disappointment knowing the glove was going to tell who killed Declan. Through DNA or some such. It seemed a little anticlimactic to me. I wanted to figure it out, not hand it over to science.

My stomach growled, reminding me that I hadn't

eaten dinner in all the chaos. Quietly I got up and started making a grilled cheese. Before long, Watson padded into the kitchen, doubtless the smell of buttered bread in the skillet wafting into his dreams. Typically I would've given him some of my grilled cheese, but I didn't want to risk any chance of constipation, just in case he'd swallowed some of the shards. Instead, I simply toasted a slice of bread and gave it to him as I ate my sandwich. His snack was gone in two bites, and then he disappeared back into the bedroom. He was eating as voraciously as normal, another good sign.

My thoughts drifted back to Declan and the Diamonds. I felt like I had missed something. Something obvious. It wasn't surprising that the glove was behind the toyshop. Well, it was, for the killer to do something so careless, but even so, it only confirmed what I already suspected. The killer was right there. But which one? The betrayed father? The brother in love with his sister-in-law? The pregnant wife who discovered her husband was cheating?

Cheating. It was one piece of the puzzle.... Sarah Margaret Beeman.

Maybe she played more of a role than just that of the other woman.

At that thought, I left my crumb-filled plate on

the kitchen counter, retrieved my laptop, and carried it back into the bedroom so I could keep an eye on Watson.

I situated myself against the headboard and propped the laptop on a couple of pillows in my lap, then opened Google and typed in Sarah Margaret Beeman. Might as well start with the simple and go from there.

I got nothing relevant, of course. There was an author with the name Margaret Beeman, an actress, a woman who worked with horses, but none close by and of an age that I thought would appeal to Declan. I narrowed it down to Colorado, still nothing.

I tried a couple of people-search websites, but they kept asking questions like—is Sarah Margaret Beeman related to so and so? Has Sarah Margaret Beeman ever lived at this address? Has Sarah Margaret Beeman ever been convicted of a felony? After hitting *I don't know* multiple times, I realized I was wasting my effort. That, and each one of them wanted me to put in a credit card number. Which I would've done if I thought it could help. But I didn't.

Even though I realized I was wasting time at this point, I also knew I wouldn't be getting any sleep with as fast as my mind was racing. So I went with it. I just typed in Sarah. Like I suspected, nothing helpful came up. Too much came up. Including a list of nicknames. I had no idea women named Sarah were also called Sadie or Sal. How odd.

Odd, but not at all helpful.

Feeling like I was wasting time, I did a similar search on Sarah's middle name, more out of desperation than anything. As with Sarah, Margaret offered up more information than could ever be useful. The third link was to Wikipedia. I hesitated with the mouse over the link. Knowing that if any of my ex-professor colleagues found out I ever clicked on Wikipedia as an actual source, they would quite literally crucify me. Well, whatever. I clicked.

I discovered that Margaret was a French name originally, and then later English. Not helpful or even overtly interesting. But then there was a long list of nicknames. A few of which I had no idea how they could possibly come from the name Margaret. The last one of those was a name I knew. *Peggy*.

I stared at the name, my blood running cold just as the tingling over my skin increased. Peggy was a nickname for Margaret. I couldn't understand why, but there it was in black-and-white. So, it made sense that Peg would be as well.

Peg. Peg Singer. Not quite Peg Beeman, but I knew I'd found it. I was willing to bet Beeman was

Peg's maiden name. Those two letters from the Denver law firm to Sarah M. Beeman. Sarah Margaret Beeman. In essence, to Peg Beeman. I was also willing to bet at least one of those had been in regards to Declan's will and the fate of the toyshop and the Diamond family. I'd quite literally handed over evidence to the killer.

Peg had killed Declan.

No sooner had the thought crossed my mind than I shook my head. It didn't make any sense. Why would Peg kill Declan for making her sole beneficiary? An image of her holding up my hoodie, nearly engulfed by the size, flitted to my mind. Peg couldn't have killed Declan. Not only did she not have the motive, but she quite literally couldn't. It would've been like a toy poodle killing a Doberman.

No, of course it wasn't Peg. It was Joe. Joe was every bit as big as Declan, bigger.

Joe had found out about the affair between his wife and Declan.

I texted Branson. *I know who killed Declan. Call me back.*

FIFTEEN

I woke up to the sun streaming through the bedroom window. I'd fallen asleep on top of the covers, and the computer upside down like a tent beside me. Watson peeked at me, only his pointy ears and chocolate eyes visible as he stood on his back legs, his two forepaws pounding on the mattress as he whined.

"For goodness' sake, Watson. Must you be so demanding every...." The night before came back to me, and I sat up straighter. Doing a little test, I lilted my voice in the same tone I often used when I said treat or walk. "Breakfast?"

Watson let out several deep, excited growls, plopped to the ground, and began to bounce on his two front paws like a bunny in his excited way.

The sight sent such relief through me I nearly cried. I slid off the bed and gathered him in my arms.

"You're feeling better! You're really going to be fine, aren't you?"

The bark he gave next was a clear admonition, and he jerked himself free, giving me a side glare, then looking toward the bedroom door and beginning to bounce again.

Laughing, I stood up. "Yes, Your Majesty. Anything you want since you're feeling better! You name it. Toast, a can of tuna? Prime rib?"

He let out two short impatient yips.

"Twice, huh? I'll take that to mean you want the second choice. Which is good. I don't actually have any prime rib." He pranced at my feet as I walked to the kitchen, nearly tripping me a billion times in the short distance. I don't think I ever enjoyed nearly falling so much.

Watson was almost through with his bowl of tuna when other aspects of the night before returned as well. I rushed back to the bedroom and snagged my phone. There was a message from Verona, and another from Katie. No missed calls, and nothing from Branson.

I called him again. Still no answer.

I considered calling the police. Susan wouldn't be back on duty this quickly, surely. But then I paused. I'd already tried the police. I'd attempted to do the responsible, regular citizen sort of thing. But it wasn't what I wanted to do.

Feeling much, much happier than I should about that, I brushed my teeth, threw on clothes, and pulled my hair into a ponytail quicker than I ever had in my life. I was so wide-awake, I didn't even need to stop at the Black Bear Roaster. Solving a murder was an even better wake-me-up than caffeine.

Still nervous to put a collar on Watson, despite him seemingly being back to normal, I carried him into the car. From his thrashing around, chances were high I was doing more damage than the collar ever would, but the die had been cast. And truly, from the way he was acting, by the time I closed the passenger door and received a murderous glare through the window, I figured the only thing I'd risked was matricide.

Just to make sure I could say that I truly had tried, I texted Branson. *I know who killed Declan. I'm on my way to get the glove. Call me back.*

I'd just started the engine when I realized what I was forgetting. I hurried back into the cabin, grabbed a gallon-sized Ziploc bag, and then Watson and I were on our way.

When I attempted to pat Watson's head, he

sniffed and turned around. Unwilling to give him the last word, I tickled his nubbed tail. He attempted to tuck it away but failed, causing me to giggle, and only dig my hole deeper.

The snow had fallen through the night, and it truly was a winter wonderland. If it had been another moment, I would've paused and enjoyed the sight of the herd of elk, steam rising from their nostrils, as I drove into town. It couldn't have been lovelier. The snow lay heavy on the branches, turning each one into a Christmas tree. The blanketing covered every building, house, and store, transforming Estes Park into a magical Christmas village as the snow sparkled in the glistening morning sun.

I giggled again at the thought, remembering the porcelain Christmas village under my grandmother's tree when I was a kid. How I'd lie on my stomach and watch the battery-powered ice-skaters twirl over the frosted-mirrored pond. Imagining what life would be like in such a magical place. It turned out, pretty murderous. At least much more than one would expect.

I giggled yet again. Watson deigned to inspect me over his shoulder. Clearing my throat, I focused on the road. Something was wrong with me that I was so excited about going to retrieve a murder weapon.

I parked just on the other side of the stream of the newly redone riverwalk. From the spot, I could see the alley that the toyshop and T-shirt place shared. I didn't attempt to pat Watson as I exited the car, though I did crack the windows slightly. He wasn't the only one who could play hard to get. "I'll be right back. You can't come on this one, but I won't be very long."

He'd been crossing the middle console onto the driver seat to hop out just as I closed the door, and once more he glared daggers at me from behind the window.

Swinging my purse on my shoulder, I left the parking lot, made my way over the little wooden bridge that crossed the narrow part of the river, and headed down the winding, mostly cleared, sandstone path. Halfway to the alley, I realized just how cold it actually was, which should have been a no-brainer, considering all the snow, but I'd been so excited I hadn't brought a coat. Whatever. I remembered the plastic bag, no... the *evidence* bag. That was much more important than being warm.

I strolled purposely across the space. There was no one about. And even if there was, I wasn't doing anything other than what people did all day long, every single day.

As I entered the alley, my heart rate increased, just a touch, despite there being no reason for concern. It was morning, bright out, and I wasn't doing anything suspicious.

Right... because I began every morning by digging through people's trash.

Standing in front of the snow-covered dumpster, which the white stuff somehow made look magical, I realized the other thing I'd forgotten. Gloves. Both for the cold in digging into the snow and to avoid my own prints from contaminating anything. Susan's voice mocked in my memory about her being the actual police.

I hated to prove her right, even for a second.

The solution was obvious enough. Retrieving the Ziploc bag from my purse, I turned it inside out, and used it for a combination glove and digging tool.

Thankfully, I didn't actually have to dig through the dumpster. The pizza Watson found had been on the side closest to the back doors. So I started sifting off snow from the right of the dumpster. I wasn't quite sure under which lump of white fluff it would be. The snow might be pretty, but it just turned everything into big, sparkling, indefinable lumps.

I dusted some off, revealing a couple of T-shirts and some broken toys. And then I found the pizza box. I had to be close. Although I couldn't remember once I'd pulled the glove out of Watson's mouth if I had flung it away. I didn't think so. I really should have tried to recreate that scene in my memory before walking into the alley.

I began to dust the snow away a little more frantically, it wasn't like the glove would break if I hit it. Something small and hard went flying and hit the back door to Rocky Mountain Imprints with a loud clank. I froze, waiting.

Nothing happened. I began flinging snow again, though with a little less vigor. An orange yo-yo went flying next, but didn't make any noise other things clattering across the ground. And then, there it was. The glove, now matted with snow and frozen stiff. I wrapped my Ziploc-gloved hand around it, picked it up, and then refolded the bag right side out, enclosing the evidence, and zipped it up in triumph. I looked at it, smiled, and gave a nod of approval. "Gotcha!"

"Fred! What are you doing?"

I jumped and let out an embarrassingly squeaky yelp, as I looked toward the voice. Peg was standing right outside the back door, her hand over her eyes as she squinted at me in the brightness.

My mouth moved silently for a second or two—or maybe an hour, who could tell?—then words came. Like magic. Totally bypassing my brain and all thought processes and spewing out of my mouth. "Watson got into something bad in here last night as we were leaving. I had to take him to the vet. Dr. Sallee suggested that if I could find out what it was, we'd have a better chance of helping him." Look at that. Not only words, but full sentences, good ones too. *Take that, Susan Green!*

"Oh, I'm so sorry, the poor dear." Peg's tone shifted from surprised to sympathy. "I hope it's nothing poisonous. I would just hate—" Her words fell away instantly, and she looked at the bag in my hands, her gaze returning to me, then back to the bag. "Fred, what have you got there?" All sympathy vanished, her tone was as cold as the snow.

Her reaction threw me off. She recognized the glove. Which meant, she knew. Obviously. But... *Peg knew?* "Just some material... um... there was some... ah... pizza sauce on it that he was eating. I thought maybe Watson had swallowed some of this...."

I was fairly certain Susan Green was laughing so hard that Peg was about to ask her to be quiet.

"Fred...." Peg took a step toward me, and I automatically backed one away from her. She paused, staring, and then to my surprise, darted back to the shop.

Relief flooded through me, though I continued backing up, feeling like I needed to keep my attention right where it was.

With a ferocity that shocked me, Peg burst back out the door. Her wild expression made it look like she should be screaming, but she wasn't. Only pure silence as she tore down the three steps, the baseball bat gripped in both hands and raised above her head as she flew toward me.

I spun on my heels and attempted to run, and slipped. Another idiotic mistake, me and my dumb cowboy boots, even in the snow. I caught myself before I fell and managed to move, just in time to feel the air brush past my head from the bat.

I ran, and I could hear her pounding footsteps right behind me. It was a losing game, and I knew it. I wouldn't be able to win a race against a sleeping hippopotamus, let alone little Peg Singer, or Sarah Margaret Beeman, whoever.... I ripped the purse off my shoulder and threw it back behind me, not bothering to look.

She let out a loud yell and there was a crash.

I dared to look back, and sure enough, she'd fallen, though I wasn't certain if it was due to getting tangled in the purse straps or simply hitting a patch of ice. Not that it mattered. No sooner had I glanced than she was getting back up. Peg started toward me, but her bat had skated away.

The tables had turned. I couldn't outrun her, but I could squash that little pixie like a bug.

She took two steps, paused, maybe seeing the expression in my eyes, and then darted back for the baseball bat.

And with that, it was back to running.

Thanks to the few yards she had to go to retrieve the bat, I made it through the trails, over the bridge, and into the car. Once more I was glad to have my burnt-orange little Mini Cooper. As long as the key was on me, which thankfully hadn't fallen out of the pocket of my broomstick skirt, the car automatically unlocked, and I pulled open the door, scaring Watson half to death. I hit Lock and slammed my foot on the brake to start the ignition.

A loud crash against the driver-side window caused both Watson and I to scream. The glass cracked in a myriad of spiderwebs, but didn't break fully. One more hit and it would. I shoved the gear in Reverse and hit the gas. As we pulled past her, Peg swung the bat again, managing to take out a headlight.

As soon as we were clear, I shifted into Drive and stomped on the gas again. I spared a glance in the rearview mirror. To my surprise, I didn't see her.

Just as I reached the end of the parking lot and started to turn onto the street, there was a loud rumble, and a huge four-by-four truck backed out between the cars.

I didn't wait to make sure. Flooring it, I zoomed onto the street, and within half a block reached the main intersection of downtown. Another glance in my rearview revealed Peg pulling out of the parking lot, her truck's rear tires fishtailing. Hitting the gas again, I took a right turn at the lights, praying no tourists were jaywalking and about to get plowed down. Luck was on our side.

For one crazy second, I couldn't think where to go, then for an even crazier one, I decided to go to my house.

Watson whimpered in the passenger seat, and I spared him a glance. "It's okay, buddy. It really is. It going to be okay."

Lies, lies, lies. Of all the injustices I'd done to Watson that morning, this was the only true one.

And then the obvious hit me. The police station.

I didn't care if Susan Green was there or not. It could be filled with fifteen billion Susan Greens, and it would still be the place to go. Now I simply needed to outmaneuver a huge four-by-four truck.

No problem. Running, I couldn't do. Drive like I was a stunt double in *The Italian Job*? Piece of cake.

Thankfully the police station was less than half a mile away, so I wouldn't have to truly test my skills for too long. I tore through the next intersection, running a red light, but it was early enough in the day that there were no cars or pedestrians in the way.

My phone rang, lighting up the center display of the Mini Cooper. Announcing Branson Wexler was calling.

Men had the best timing.

I hit Accept on the steering wheel as I whipped around a spot of ice glistening in the sunlight.

"Fred. I'm so sorry. I just saw your messages. What—"

"Shut up!" I was aware of my screaming, and I was also aware that there was no other way I could do it right then. Poor Watson was howling in the passenger seat. "I'm bringing Peg into the station, right now. She's the killer, I think. At least she's trying to kill me."

"What are you—"

"I said shut up!" I could see the police station now, coming up on the left. "I'm almost there. If you're in there, come outside. If not, call them and let them know I'm coming." What a ridiculous thing to say. Like I was going to wait on Branson to come get me from the car, or that he'd have time to call if he wasn't there before I came peeling in.

Peg's engine roared behind us. I spared another glance and saw the massive chrome of her grill growing larger. Another ten seconds and she'd plow right over us.

"Fred, slow down. You're not making—"

"Shut up!" Without a moment to spare, we reached the turnoff to the police station. I cranked the wheel to the left, and was airborne for a second as I hit the curb. Watson let out another loud, mournful howl.

Although probably stupid, I spared a second glance, and saw Peg's truck zoom by, then noticed her making a similar motion on the steering wheel, and the truck began to turn, once again fishtailing and nearly going out of control.

I slammed the car into Park right in front of the police station doors, managing to dart my hand out just in time to keep Watson seated, then scooped him up, grabbed the glove, and darted from my car.

Branson was saying something over the speakers.

Watson was so frazzled, he didn't even resist.

"Help!" I burst through the front doors of the police station, scaring the officer at the front desk, judging from the cup of coffee that went flying. "She's trying to kill us."

Just as I reached the desk, I turned around in time to see Peg's truck fly past the police station.

I pointed after her and looked over at the wide-eyed officer. "You're probably going to wanna chase her down."

SIXTEEN

"Merry Christmas Eve Eve." Branson held up his glass of wine between us and waited patiently for the awkwardly long amount of time it took me to realize I needed to raise my own glass in cheers.

"Merry Christmas Eve Eve." I clinked our glasses together, and then we both took a sip. I wasn't a wine connoisseur, but this was better than any I'd had before, full of earthiness and spice. A perfect holiday wine. Considering it was about three hundred a bottle, it should have tasted like gold. It wasn't that good.

Branson set his wineglass down, interlaced his fingers, and propped his elbows on the tabletop. "You seem distracted, everything okay?"

I knew the correct answer was *Yes, I am fine, just a little flustered from Watson and I nearly being run over earlier that morning.* Instead I was honest. "I feel a little out of place. I've driven by here several times, and judging from the outside and the name, I never would've guessed it was so fancy in here." The candlelit interior of shiny dark wood and brushed steel reminded me of some of the more exclusive restaurants on the Plaza.

"Well, I will admit that the name *Pasta Thyme* doesn't overly evoke a fine-dining expectation." His gaze traveled over me. Not uncomfortably, but only heightening my lack of preparation and appearance. "Trust me, Fred, you're the furthest thing from out of place. You look beautiful."

No, I didn't. The one thing I had going for me was Percival's lessons about dramatic cat eye and a subtle lip gloss. Other than that, I looked like I did every other day. Tangerine peasant blouse, faded turquoise broomstick skirt, and white cowboy boots. At least the boots had silver tips on the toes to match my dangling silver earrings. Thank goodness, I'd managed to actually put on earrings again. I hadn't even done anything with my hair, just left it flowing free, though I was fairly certain I combed it.

Branson, on the other hand, was the epitome of beauty. He could've stepped out of any movie from the fifties. I was on a date with Rock Hudson in a classic black suit, cranberry shirt, and an emerald-green tie. A Rock Hudson, who was evidently truly interested in me and not secretly wondering if I had a brother at home.

No, not a date. After wrapping up with Peggy that afternoon, Branson had called and suggested we get dinner and he'd fill me in on how everything had worked out.

A tuxedoed waiter appeared from thin air with some silver scraper thing and dusted breadcrumbs from the tablecloth around my plate. He didn't have to do that for Branson—none of his crumbs had made a run for it.

Tuxedoed waiter.

Suit-clad Rock Hudson.

In the center of the table was a small yet lavish bouquet of a solitary poinsettia bloom in the midst of sprigs of holy and silver sticks.

Yeah, date. Whether I wanted it to be that or not.

I couldn't bring myself to respond to the 'me looking beautiful' comment, so I turned things to where I was the most comfortable. "So, she admitted it? Peg was the one who actually killed Declan?"

"She did." If Branson was disappointed in the shift of the conversation, he didn't let on.

"She admitted to both? Attacking him at the toy store and at the hospital?"

"Sure did."

"Huh." Ridiculously, disappointment flitted through me. I hated being wrong.

Apparently my emotions were on my sleeve, and Branson chuckled. "You thought it was her husband?"

"I did. I thought he found out about their affair. And I couldn't imagine little Peg being able or strong enough to hurt Declan to begin with." Thoughts of my poor beat-up Mini Cooper flashed through my mind, causing me to let out a chuckle. "Although, now I understand how she was able to get all those softball trophies. She's got quite an arm."

"That she does." Branson took another sip of wine. "I'm actually surprised that poor wooden nutcracker was in one piece from how hard she can swing. It was no wonder Declan was in a coma."

That part had been bugging me all day. "So why the garland? If she'd already hit him, why stop?"

He tilted his glass of wine toward me. "You've got a sharp mind, Fred. You really do. I asked her that myself. She wasn't able to give an answer. I don't think even she understood it. But my guess is our little Peg Singer, or Sarah Margaret Beeman, doesn't really have the heart of a killer. Hitting someone once is one thing, bashing them repeatedly is another. And though I'm sure she didn't account for that garland to end up so bloodied, using it to strangle is a little less visceral than beating her lover to death. As for what she did at the hospital? She could've smothered him with a pillow, but putting air in his line, she didn't even have to touch him."

It made sense. Although she seemed more than willing to bash me to death with that baseball bat. Then again, she and I hadn't been having an affair.

The waiter returned and refilled my glass of wine. I hadn't realized I'd drank it so fast. It went down smoothly, too smoothly, and I was nervous, not a good combo. I started to take another sip and then pushed it away. I didn't drink very often, which meant I was a lightweight, and I was going to stay in control on this date, or whatever it was.

Somehow the emerald of Branson's tie caused the green of his eyes to nearly glow.

I pushed the wine a little farther away. "And Joe didn't know?"

For the first time, Branson winced. "That was the hardest part of the day. I'll admit, it's difficult to see a man like Joe, one so big and strong, completely break. He was devastated. He didn't know about the affair. Not a good Christmas for him. Discovering his wife had been cheating and that he was married to a murderer all in one fell swoop."

I hadn't even considered that. And I'd thought discovering Garrett's affair and ending our marriage had been bad. At least he hadn't been a murderer or a dirty cop.

I'd have to go check on Joe. Let him know…. Let him know what? That was a stupid impulse. I was certain I would be the last person he'd want to see. "Did she explain why she killed Declan? Why she attacked him to begin with? I can't understand."

Another wince. "Peg remained steadfast for over an hour in her interview. Wouldn't admit to anything. Then I brought Joe in. Everything fell apart in that moment, for both of them. And fell into place for me." He leveled his gaze on mine. "Affair aside, she loved her husband. She really did. The minute he broke, so did she. And if I had any doubts left about her being able to kill Declan, her fury at him, even still, would have convinced me." He paused as the waiter returned to refill our waters. "She'd tried to end their affair. But Declan wouldn't have it. He was convinced she was going to leave Joe, which, I think had been the original plan, though Peg never fully admitted to that part. That's why Declan was going to leave Daphne. He truly believed he and Peg were going to be together. It seems he was almost delusional about it. That's why he'd done the documents in her maiden name. He was that certain she was leaving Joe. When Peg got the updated version of Declan's will, it was the last straw. It sent her into some sort of rage."

Horror washed over me. "That's what did it? Her reading the will?"

Branson nodded, his gaze concerned. "Yes. Why?"

I took a steadying breath and gripped the edge of the table. "I think I'm the one who gave her that. A couple of letters had been misdelivered to me. It seems that happens all the time. Both of them were from a Denver law firm."

Branson reached across the table, placed his hand over mine, and gave a gentle squeeze. "None of this is your fault, Fred. You just returned the letter to where it was sent."

I realized that of course, but still, it was like I'd placed the nutcracker in Peg's hand.

The waiter arrived, sliding our plates of food in

front of us, then grating fresh Parmesan over the tops.

I glowered at my plate of creamy sausage tagliatelle. The dish had been thirty dollars, and the portion was roughly half the size of a bowl of spaghetti anywhere else.

"You're going to die when you taste this." Branson smiled at me, then plunged his fork into one of his gnocchi. Thankfully he hadn't seemed to notice my reaction.

Following suit, I skewered a thick noodle and swirled it, then took a bite. I shuddered, literally. I glanced down at my plate in shock, then back up at Branson.

"Told you." His grin turned wicked. "All the pasta is housemade. I'm only going to take you to the best places, Fred."

I was speechless, both to his statement and in the pure divine that was happening in my mouth. The wine was most definitely not worth three hundred dollars, but I would've paid thirty dollars a bite, if need be, to experience the pasta again.

Both because I couldn't think of a response to his claim and being completely overwhelmed by flavor, I made some sort of awkward sound of agreement and took another bite. It was just as good as the first.

The next several minutes were lost to the pleasure of food and the discovery of their garlic bread, also housemade, rivaling the pasta. Gradually, thoughts of Peg began to tumble over the exquisiteness of the meal and my nerves around Branson.

"I think the only other thing I don't understand is the glove. Why in the world would she be so careless just to toss it by the dumpster in the alley outside her store?"

Branson chewed a few more seconds, swallowed, then wiped his mouth, though it hadn't seemed to need it. "Katie truly did interrupt her. Peg dashed out the back of the toy store, tossed the glove, and hurried into the T-shirt shop, just in case whoever had interrupted her came into her store to get help. It would've been a fairly perfect alibi." He shrugged and gave an almost sympathetic wince. "But Peg said she went back to find it and couldn't. Finally decided an animal had carried it off. Personally, that's the one part of the story I don't understand. If it were me, I would've torn that place apart. There's no way I would've missed finding those gloves." He shrugged again, just one shoulder that time. "Although, we tore it apart this afternoon, and we never found the second one."

Despite the situation, I laughed a little. "I can see

that. I don't know how many times I've lost my keys or my cell phone, and nearly destroyed the house in the search only to find them in the exact place I'd looked countless times before."

"Maybe so, but your keys or cell phone couldn't help prove that you'd murdered someone."

"True." I really could understand that happening. "Just more proof that I shouldn't go around killing people. Something like that would totally happen to me."

Branson snorted, and somehow made the garish noise sound classy. "Really? You have a hit list going that I should know about?"

I shook my head, though Officer Green flitted through my mind. As did my ex-husband and my ex-best friend turned ex-business partner. No, those two flitted away instantly. It was thanks to them that I'd made the choices I did and ended up in Estes Park, and I was grateful for that. It took a little more effort to erase Susan's name from the list, however. "No. I don't commit murders. I just solve them." I couldn't help myself.

Branson didn't laugh. If anything, I could've sworn his gaze grew a little heated. "That you do, Winifred Page. That you do."

I plunged my fork back to the plate, ready to

twirl around more noodles, only to discover it was empty. Branson must've seen the disappointment over my face as he laughed. I grinned up at him sheepishly. "Don't you hate it when you don't realize that you're done and go for that last, delicious bite only to discover you've already had it?"

He winked. "Their portions aren't exactly huge. We can order a second round."

Santa help me, but I almost said yes. Then remembered I had some pride. "No, that portion was perfect."

Branson's eyes narrowed. "You're aware I can tell when you lie to me, right?"

"I don't know what you're talking about."

"Sure you don't." He took his final bite, chewed, swallowed, and then needlessly wiped his mouth again. "Dessert, then. They're simple and unfussy, but their tiramisu and cannoli are the best I've ever had."

I could only imagine the price tag on those, and I felt the sting of guilt at realizing how much Branson was going to pay for a night he considered a date and one that I was unwilling to label. But the best tiramisu and cannoli he'd ever had? I couldn't say no to that. And as guilty as I felt about leaving Watson at home, without him here, I wouldn't have to share.

Branson ordered the desserts, and though I couldn't tell what words he was about to say, there was a spark, a change in his demeanor, and I couldn't let him go wherever he was about to go.

"So where were you? I tried to call and text last night and this morning." I smiled to let him know I wasn't angry and tried to include in the expression an apology for stopping whatever was about to happen the second before. "Not that you need to stay by your phone for me, but I truly did try to do the right, proper citizen sort of thing."

What I thought was disappointment flitted across his face, but it was gone quickly, and when he laughed, it didn't sound forced. "You're not attempting to cause me to feel bad for making it possible for this whole thing to go exactly how you would've wanted."

He really did have my number. "I didn't imply anything of the kind, and I definitely didn't say you needed to feel bad. I was merely asking. You just got back from being out of town for a couple of weeks, on a trip you said wasn't exactly a vacation, but not exactly work. Same thing last night and this morning?"

For the first time, he looked uncomfortable, and maybe a touch... panicked? Whatever it was, it was gone in a flash and his easy charm returned. "Yes. Something like that again."

I waited for a second, thinking he was going to continue, then realized that was the only answer I was going to get. Which was fine. He didn't owe me one, especially since we weren't on a date. Even if we kind of were.

But for whatever reason, that hesitation allowed a thought of Leo, his warm, honey-brown eyes, and his deep, soft voice to flash into my mind.

Nope. That wasn't happening either.

"And you're right, Sergeant Wexler. I'm glad things went down just as they did." For whatever reason, it seemed like I was mostly an open book to Branson, so I only hesitated for a second before deciding to ask what I really wanted to know. "Did you happen to run into Officer Green today? I was wondering if she had any... thoughts about the situation."

He chuckled, this time the sound fully heated, and there was that spark again. "You might be on the right side of the law and have an uncanny knack for solving murders, Fred, but you've got just a touch of wickedness in you."

I shook my head. "Not true. Not at all. Just ask my mother. She'll tell you."

"Then she'd be wrong." Branson once more lifted his glass of wine my way. "And I'm glad of it."

Before he'd finished his sip, our tiramisu and cannoli were delivered. And I discovered that if I'd been willing to pay thirty dollars a bite for the pasta, I'd have to triple that for the desserts.

SEVENTEEN

Watson and I spent Christmas Eve finishing the nonfiction room. Watson didn't so much shelve books as nap, snore, and occasionally beg for treats, but just having him act fully like himself was more than enough help. Katie kept calling from Denver, wanting more measurements on the floor space of the kitchen. I had a feeling she was spending a small fortune—possibly a gargantuan fortune—on equipment. Percival and Gary brought down the Victorian sofa and lamp and arranged them by the river rock fireplace. Even though I hadn't started on shelving any of the mystery books, it was the only confirmation I needed to prove that it truly was going to be my favorite nook in the store.

By the time the sun set at a little after four in the afternoon and the streetlamps and Christmas lights twinkled on outside the window, I finally got up the nerve to do what had been in the back of my mind all day.

Remembering my coat and gloves, and feeling safe enough to not only put a collar and leash back around Watson's neck but also a green snowflake-patterned scarf, we made our way up the street, and with a deep breath, walked into Bushy Evergreen's Workshop.

As before, the smells of Christmas filled the toyshop, and somehow left me feeling cozy, even though I was intimately aware of what had happened in that cheerful place. The piped-in music played a soft version of "Baby, It's Cold Outside." The only things different were the lack of the sparkling garland and the lack of a handsome man at the counter.

Dolan and Daphne smiled a greeting from their place behind the counter as Watson and I rounded a tall tower of toys and came into view. Both of their smiles faltered for just a second but quickly slid back into place. Dolan's hand was covering Daphne's, and even when I noticed, they didn't pull apart.

"Hi. I needed to do some last-minute Christmas shopping." I couldn't seem to get a handle on my nerves. "Is it okay if I do that here?"

Dolan's smile changed, becoming a little more sincere, and though he would never be a head turner, I could see what everyone had meant. There was such genuine kindness and gentleness, that in truth, he was twice as attractive as his brother. "You'll always be welcome at Bushy's. We're in your debt."

It took me a second to figure out what to say. I most definitely hadn't expected that. "No. You're really not."

Daphne shook her stunningly beautiful head. "Yes, we are. Sergeant Wexler made it very clear that it was you who figured things out. Believe me, we were very aware of what everyone thought had happened."

I made a mental note to thank Branson for not mentioning that I too suspected them of killing Declan. "I lucked into it more than anything." I nodded down at Watson. "Really, it was his penchant for constantly looking for food that discovered the missing puzzle piece. Not me."

The sound of a throat being cleared caused all three of us to look toward the rear of the store. Old Duncan Diamond shuffled from the back and held something out to me. He didn't smile, and it was clear from his bloodshot eyes that he'd spent countless hours over the past several days weeping. "I thought it was you. I made you this to say—" His voice broke, and he gave a small shake of his outstretched hand.

I took the object he offered, held it up for inspection, and gasped. The carved figurine was less than two inches tall and three inches long but a near-perfect replica of Watson. It was unpainted, but had been varnished a shiny golden brown.

Percival and Gary had filled me in on the gossip when they delivered the furniture. Declan's will had left everything to Peg. But considering the circumstances, Joe had Gerald Jackson give it back over to Duncan. Gerald had handled the paperwork, so of course, Percival and Gary somehow thought he'd worked a miracle.

I stared at the beautiful corgi in my hand and felt my eyes burn. I didn't deserve it. It was clear they felt they owed me a thanks for giving them their life back.

They didn't.

Knowing that if I said anything to Duncan the tears really would come, I knelt and held the figurine out to Watson. "Look, buddy. It's you."

He sniffed it, then gave it a quick lick. For him, that was the height of being impressed.

I stood back up and clutched it to my heart, and

though it was a horrible thought, I felt like Duncan had given me something that ensured I would always have Watson with me, forever. My gaze met his, and I attempted to say thank you, but failed.

His lips turned into a small, sad smile.

He understood.

I sniffed and glanced over at Daphne and Dolan, just in time to catch Dolan pulling his hand away from where it had rested on Daphne's flat stomach. And though it was only a hunch, I would've bet everything that the father of Daphne's baby was right there in that shop.

Just when I thought I was going to lose it and actually start to cry, the piped-in music switched, and a version of "Jingle Bells" with dog barks auto-tuned to match the melody began to play. Watson barked along, loudly and utterly off-key.

And the spell broke, which was both a little sad and a relief.

Daphne smiled, and her voice was soft and content. "I believe you said you had some Christmas shopping to do?"

"We're having to pull the garland from the market. There are over fifteen lawsuits pending." Noah had the audacity to sound baffled as he lamented to Barry while the men set the table for the Christmas meal. Mom and the twins were both cooking away in the kitchen. They'd kicked me out over an hour ago. So, as normal, I was with the boys.

Jonah sounded just as flummoxed. "We even had on the packaging to wear gloves. It's like people don't know how to read."

"Yes, it's the most shocking thing I've ever heard." Percival rolled his eyes and gave a stage whisper to Gary. "Who would ever think Christmas decorations that could double for murder weapons you might find in a game of Clue would ever lead to litigation?"

Looking utterly offended, Noah opened his mouth to retort, but I jumped in quickly. "Could the lawsuits hurt you? Take your homes or anything?" As much as I'd ended up despising that garland, I knew they'd never had any malintent.

Jonah scoffed and waved away the concern as if it was nothing. "Nah. Our insurance is good. And our lineup of products we're launching starting in January is strong enough that even if the lawsuits are more than we anticipated, we'll be fine."

"Well, I loved it." Barry shook his head empathetically. "But we had to get rid of it. Anything that hurt Watson has to go." He turned and squatted down, making eye contact with Watson, who'd been sleeping across the room. "Don't we, boy? You come first, don't you?" Barry's Christmas outfit consisted of a red-and-green tie-dyed tank top with a penguin wearing reindeer antlers on the front, over baggie fuchsia-and-orange tie-dyed yoga pants. I wasn't sure if it was the clashing combination or his hairy back showing from the tank top as he held out his arms toward Watson that caused my eyes to burn.

It seemed that dogs truly were colorblind, as Watson sprang from his nap and launched himself at rocket speed into Barry's arms.

In the corner of the room, by the Christmas tree now decorated with boring everyday garland, my four nieces and nephews played with their new toys, each electronic. They'd been allowed to open one when they arrived, the rest would come after the feast. I almost hated for them to open what I brought. I couldn't imagine any of them were going to be overly excited about all the hand-carved toys they were about to receive. Maybe when they got home, they'd toss them in a chest, forget about them, and in thirty years discover them again and see them as timeless heirlooms. Maybe.

Mom popped her head out of the kitchen,

glanced around, then spotted me. "Dear, would you call Katie again? If she's much later, dinner is going to get cold. We're just about ready."

"I called her less than five minutes ago, Mom. She said she would be here soon." Mom was insanely easygoing, except for when she cooked. It was time to eat as soon as it was ready. It was hot and fresh, or not at all. "If need be, we can start before she gets here."

"Never. Not in a million years would we do that to lovely Katie." Mom looked scandalized. She disappeared back into the kitchen, but her voice carried over the Christmas carols playing in the background. "But call her again, would you?"

I was the one who'd opted to move back to be with family.

Acquiescing, I lifted my cell. At that moment, there was a knock on the door. I hurried over and threw it open. "Thank goodness. My mother was about to turn me into your stalker."

"Sorry about that. I just couldn't force myself to quit decorating this morning." She held up a tray covered with a silver dome that had melted snowflakes trailing down its etched surface. She shoved it toward me. "Take this, will you? But don't drop it or make it too off-center, I spent hours on that thing."

"Oh, great. No pressure." I took the tray, which was lighter than it appeared.

Katie shut the door behind her, and hurried over to me. I'd been carrying it to the kitchen, but she stopped me in the middle of the living room. "Here, I can't wait for you to see." Without any warning, she lifted the lid with a flourish and revealed her dessert.

"A gingerbread house! It's..." Confusion flitted through me, then I understood. For the second time in less than twenty-four hours, I gasped and felt my eyes stinging. "Oh, Katie. It's... just perfect."

It was a gingerbread *dog*house, the sides slanted to form a hexagon shape, with an arched doorway in the front outlined in peppermints. Little candies shaped like red balls rimmed the four edges of the house while multicolored, sugarcoated jelly-orange slices framed the outline of the front. A little green wreath complete with red berries of icing hung over the doorway. Snow piled up around the golden foil landscape and on the roof as icicles hung delicately from the edge. A small path curved from the open front door, lined with more red candies and... I cocked my head as one more detail snapped into place.

"Are those dog bones?" Percival sounded scandalized.

A second later Barry let out a gasp of his own and clapped his hands. "They are!"

Sure enough dog bones standing on end made a fence of sorts leading up the curved path and also outlined the edges of the roof.

Gary was nearby and walked over as he let out a low whistle, then gave an appreciative glance toward Katie. "Girl, if that's any indication, you're going to make a fortune in that bakery or yours." He raised his voice. "Phyllis, Verona, Zelda, get out here. You've gotta see this."

"Not if she puts dog treats on her desserts." Though I was fairly certain that Percival had meant to whisper, his comment earned him a swift elbow in the side from Gary.

For once, Mom quit worrying about getting dinner on the table as soon as it was done. And for several minutes, the entire family gathered around the gingerbread doghouse, oohing, aahing, and lavishing endless praise on Katie.

She was as red as any light-up nose on Rudolph I'd ever seen, and looked utterly pleased. "Show Watson. It's in honor of him, obviously."

"Watson." I knelt as I called him over.

As ever, when he knew I had food in hand, he rushed over like he lived to do my bidding.

I held it out to him, close enough that it was on my level, but far enough away that no dog hair could fix itself to the icing.

He stared at it, wide-eyed, gave a sniff, and then lunged, taking out a good fourth of the gingerbread doghouse and several of the dog treat fence posts with one shark-like bite.

The entire family screamed, and I stood quickly, trying to get it out of harm's way as if the damage hadn't already been done. Totally guilt ridden, I turned to Katie. "I'm so, so sorry."

If anything, her smile had gotten bigger, and she beamed. "Good! He liked it!"

Mom gaped at her. "Sweetheart, we all love Watson, but you spent forever on that."

Katie's brows knitted, and she looked utterly baffled as she glanced from Mom to me. "No, that was for Watson. Obviously I'm not going to serve you dog treats." She gestured with her thumb toward the door. "I made decorated gingerbread men, lemon meringue pie, and a pumpkin-carrot cake for the rest of us. It's all out in the car."

"Hallelujah and Merry Christmas, Tiny Tim!" Percival raised his hand in the air. "After a meal that includes a meatless roast, which might be worse than actual dog bones, I'm going to be craving a dessert smorgasbord!" He threw his arm around Katie. "Welcome to the family. You're stuck with us! Unless you used some kind of sugar substitute, then you're out."

TWISTER SISTERS MYSTERIES

COMING EARLY 2022

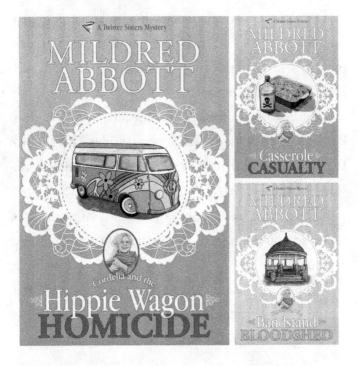

I can't begin to tell you how excited I am to finally bring this series to life. It's been in the planning and dreaming stages for over three years. The process was interrupted by my cancer diagnosis and all that came with it. A blessing in disguise, as the characters have kept me company over these years and have grown richer, deeper, and are producing a limited series (10 books in total) that is so much better than if things had gone according to *my* plan.

The Twister Sisters takes place in the charming Ozark town of Willow Lane. You've actually already met our three lead characters in the knitting group that crashed Percival and Gary's anniversary at Baldpate Inn in *Killer Keys* (the book where Fred and Leo shared their first kiss)!

You'll follow along with Cordelia, Wanda, and Pamela as they deliver their casseroles (Meals-on-Wheels style) and just happen to... you guessed it... solve murders!

The first three books are already up for pre-order, so you don't have to worry about missing their arrival!

And... this doesn't mean the end for the Cozy Corgi. Trust me, Fred—and even Watson—are cheering on their friends in their new adventure.

While Twister Sisters is a limited series, the Cozy Corgi is not. There's plenty of shenanigans ahead for our Scooby Gang.

Twister Sisters Mysteries

Katie's Gingerbread recipe provided by:

2716 Welton St Denver, CO 80205

(720) 708-3026

Click the links for more Rolling Pin deliciousness:

RollingPinBakeshop.com

Rolling Pin Facebook Page

Katie's Gingerbread Recipe

Ingredients:

    3 cups flour

    1 teaspoon baking soda

    ¾ teaspoon cinnamon

    ¾ teaspoon ginger

    ½ teaspoon allspice

    ½ teaspoon cloves

    ½ teaspoon salt

    4 ounces butter

    ¼ cup shortening

    ½ cup brown sugar

    2/3 cup molasses (7 ounces)

    1 egg

Directions:

1. Sift all dry ingredients together, set aside.
2. Cream butter, shortening, and brown sugar until light in color.
3. Add molasses and combine.
4. Add egg. Be sure to scrape edges of bowl between each addition.

5. Add dry ingredient in three stages. Be sure to mix well between each addition.

6. Chill dough for about an hour.

7. Preheat oven to 375.

8. Roll out dough and cut to desired pattern for gingerbread house.

9. Bake for about 15 minutes until firm.

10. Assemble cooled gingerbread pieces using royal icing and candies of your choice.

PATREON

Mildred Abbott's Patreon Page

Mildred Abbott is now on Patreon! By becoming a member, you gain access to exclusive Cozy Corgi merchandise, get a look behind the scenes of book creation, and receive real-life writing updates, plans, and puppy photos (becuase, of course there will be puppy photos!). You can also gain access to ebooks and recipes before publication, read future works *literally* as they are being written chapter by chapter, and can even choose to become a character in one of the novels!

Wether you choose to be a villager, busybody, police officer, super sleuth, or the fuzzy four-legged star of the show himself, please come check the

Mildred Abbott Patreon community and discover what fun awaits.

Personal Note: Being an indie writer means that some months bills are paid without much stress, while other months threaten the ability to continue the dream of writing. Becoming a member ensures that there will continue to be new Mildred Abbott books. Your support is unbelievably appreciated and invaluable.

*While there are many perks to becoming a patron, if you are a reader who can't afford to support (or simply don't feel led), rest assured you will *not* miss out on any writing. All books will continue to be published just as they always have been. None of the Mildred Abbott books will become exclusive to a select few. In fact, patrons help ensure that writing will continue to be published for everyone.

Mildred Abbott's Patreon Page

AUTHOR NOTE

Dear Reader:

Thank you so much for reading *Traitorous Toys*. If you enjoyed Fred and Watson's adventure, I would greatly appreciate a review on Amazon and Goodreads. Please drop me a note on Facebook or on my website (MildredAbbott.com) whenever you like. I'd love to hear from you.

And don't miss book three, Bickering Bird, coming January 2018. Keeping turning the page for sneak peek!

Much love, Mildred

PS: I'd also love it if you signed up for my newsletter. That way you'll never miss a new release. You won't hear from me more than once a month, nobody needs that many newsletters!

Newsletter link: Mildred Abbott Newsletter Signup

ACKNOWLEDGMENTS

A special thanks to Agatha Frost, who gave her blessing and her wisdom. If you haven't already, you simply MUST read Agatha's Peridale Cafe Cozy Mystery series. They are absolute perfection.

The biggest and most heartfelt gratitude to Katie Pizzolato, for her belief in my writing career and being the inspiration for the character of the same name in this series. Thanks to you, Katie, our beloved baker, has completely stolen both mine and Fred's heart!

Desi, I couldn't imagine an adventure without you by my side. A.J. Corza, you have given me the corgi covers of my dreams. A huge, huge thank you to all of the lovely souls who proofread the ARC versions of Cruel Candy and helped me look somewhat literate (in completely random order): Ann Attwood, Meghan Maslow, Melissa Brus, Cinnamon, Janie Beaton, Kristell Harmse, Ron Perry, Rob Andresen-Tenace, Terri Grooms, Michael Bailey, Kelly Miller, TL Travis, Jill Wexler, Patrice, Lucy Campbell, Chris Dancer, Natalie Rivieccio, A.C. Mink, Rebecca Cartee, Becca Waldrop, and Sue Paulsen. Thank you all, so very, very much!

A further and special thanks to some of my dear readers and friends who support my passion: Andrea Johnson, Fiona Wilson, Katie Pizzolato, Maggie Johnson, Marcia Gleason, Rob Andresen- Tenace, Robert Winter, Jason R., Victoria Smiser, Kristi Browning, and those of you who wanted to remain anonymous. You make a huge, huge difference in my life and in my ability to continue to write. I'm humbled and grateful beyond belief! So much love to you all!

ALSO BY MILDRED ABBOTT

-the Cozy Corgi Cozy Mystery Series-

Cruel Candy

Traitorous Toys

Bickering Birds

Savage Sourdough

Scornful Scones

Chaotic Corgis

Quarrelsome Quartz

Wicked Wildlife

Malevolent Magic

Killer Keys

Perilous Pottery

Ghastly Gadgets

Meddlesome Money

Precarious Pasta

Evil Elves

Phony Photos

Despicable Desserts

Chattering Chipmunks

Vengeful Vellum

Wretched Wool

Jaded Jewels

Yowling Yetis

Lethal Lace

Book 24 (*untitled*) - Summer 2022

(Books 1-10 are also available in audiobook format, read to perfection by Angie Hickman.)

-the Twister Sisters Mystery Series-

Starting early 2022

Hippie Wagon Homicide

Casserole Casualty

Bandstand Bloodshed

-Cozy Corgi Merchandise-

now available at:

the Cozy Corgi store at Cafe Press

Printed in the USA
CPSIA information can be obtained
at www.ICGtesting.com
LVHW041611011224
798044LV00008B/145